THE ILLUSTRATED TREASURY OF
FAIRY TALES

Designed by Rita Marshall

CREATIVE
PAPER BACKS

Illustrations © 1984 Etienne Delessert for *Beauty & the Beast*

Illustrations © 1983 Roberto Innocenti for *Cinderella*

Illustrations © 1983 Monique Felix for *Hansel & Gretel*

Illustrations © 1984 Ivan Chermayeff for *The Three Languages*

Illustrations © 1983 John Howe for *The Fisherman & His Wife*

Illustrations © 1984 Philippe Dumas for *The Queen Bee*

Illustrations © 1983 Seymour Chwast for *Bushy Bride*

Illustrations © 1984 John Collier for *The Sleeping Beauty*

Illustrations © 1984 Jacques Tardi for *The Enchanted Pig*

Illustrations © 1983 Marcel Imsand and
Rita Marshall for *The Fir Tree*

Published in 2007 by Creative Paperbacks
P.O. Box 227, Mankato, MN 56002 USA
Creative Paperbacks is an imprint of The Creative Company
Designed by Rita Marshall

ISBN 978-1-56846-144-1 (hardcover)
ISBN 978-0-89812-528-3 (pbk)
Library of Congress Control Number: 2001135669

First Paperback Edition   5   4   3   2   1

Contents

Beauty & the Beast

Madame d'Aulnoy

illustrated by Etienne Delessert

ONCE UPON A TIME

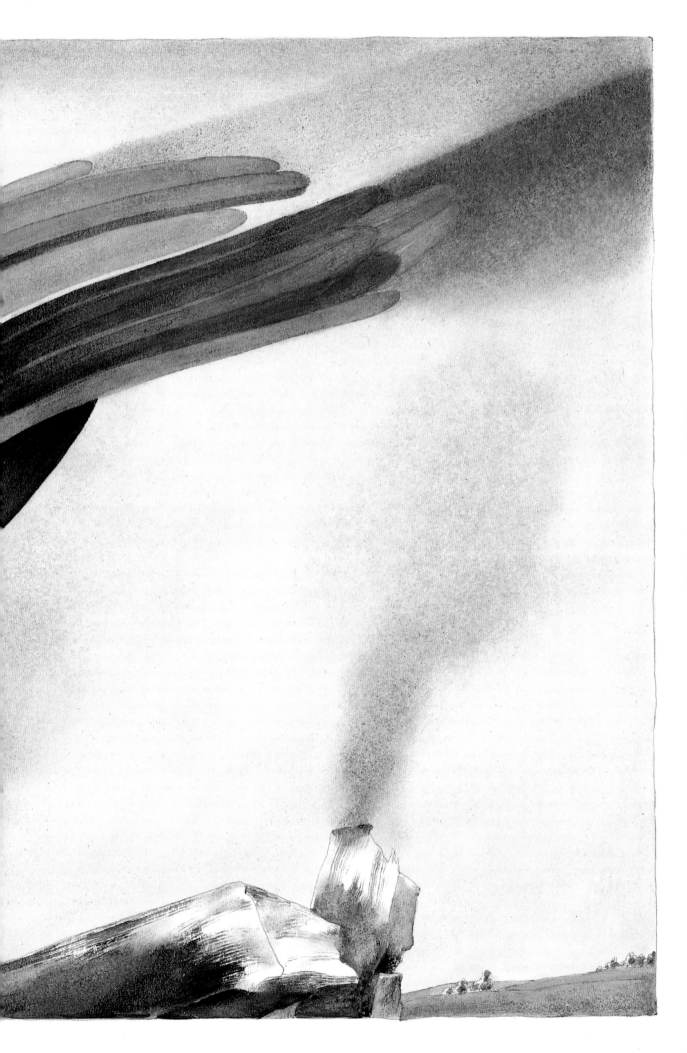

IN A VERY far-off country, there lived a merchant who had been so fortunate in all his undertakings that he was enormously rich. Even though he had six sons and six daughters, he found that his money was enough to let them all have everything they fancied, as they were accustomed to do.

But one day a most unexpected misfortune befell them. Their house caught fire and was speedily burnt to the ground, with all the splendid furniture, the books, pictures, gold, silver, and precious goods it contained. And this was only the beginning of their troubles. The father, who had until this moment prospered in all ways, suddenly lost every ship he had upon the sea, either to pirates, shipwreck, or fire. Then he heard that his clerks in distant countries, whom he trusted entirely, had proved unfaithful; and at last from great wealth he fell into the direst poverty.

All that he had left was a little house in a desolate place at least a hundred leagues from the town in which he had lived, and to this he was forced to retreat with his children, who were in despair at the idea of leading such a different life. Indeed, the daughters at first hoped that their friends, who had been so numerous while they were rich, would insist they stay in their houses now that they no longer possessed one. But they soon found that they were left alone, and that their former friends even attributed their misfortunes to their own extravagance, and showed no intention of offering them any help.

So nothing was left for them but to take their departure to the cottage, which stood in the midst of a dark forest and seemed to be the most dismal place upon the face of the earth.

As they were too poor to have any servants, the girls had to work hard, like peasants, and the sons, for their part, cultivated the fields to earn their living. Roughly clothed, and living in the simplest way, the girls missed unceasingly the luxuries and amusements of their former life. Only the youngest tried to be brave and cheerful. She had been as sad as anyone when misfortune first overtook her father, but, soon recovering her natural gaiety, she set to work to make the best of things, to amuse her father and brothers as well as she could, and to try to persuade her sisters to join her in dancing and singing. But they would do nothing of the sort, and because she was not as doleful as themselves, they declared that this miserable life was all she was fit for. But she was really far prettier and cleverer than they were. Indeed, she was so lovely that she was always called Beauty.

After two years, when they were all beginning to get used to their new life, something happened to disturb their tranquillity. Their father received the news that one of his ships, which he had believed to be lost, had come safely into port with a rich cargo. All the sons and daughters at once thought that their poverty was at an end and wanted to set out directly for the town. But their father, who was more prudent, begged them to wait a little, and, though it was harvest time and he could ill be spared, determined to go himself first, to make inquiries. Only the youngest daughter had any doubt that they would soon again be as rich as they were before, or at least rich enough to live comfortably in some town where they would find amusement and companions once more. So they all loaded their father with requests for jewels and dresses which it would have taken a fortune to buy. Only Beauty, feeling sure that it was of no use, did not ask for anything. Her father, noticing her silence, said:

"And what shall I bring for you, Beauty?"

"The only thing I wish for is to see you come home safely," she answered.

But this reply vexed her sisters, who fancied she was blaming them for having asked for such costly things. Her father, however, was pleased, but as he thought that at her age she certainly ought to like pretty presents, he told her to choose something.

"Well, dear father," she said, "as you insist upon it, I beg that you will bring me a rose. I have not seen one since we came here, and I love them so much."

So the merchant set out and reached the town as quickly as possible, only to find that his former companions, believing him to be dead, had divided between them the goods which the ship had brought. After six months of trouble and expense, he found himself as poor as when he started, having been able to recover only just enough to pay the cost of his journey. To make matters worse, he was obliged to leave the town in the most terrible weather, so that by the time he was within a few leagues of his home he was almost exhausted with cold and fatigue. Though he knew it would take some hours to get through the forest, he was so anxious to be at his journey's end that he resolved to go on. But night overtook him, and the deep snow and bitter frost made it impossible for his horse to carry him any further. Not a house was to be seen; the only shelter he could get was the hollow trunk of a great tree, and there he crouched all the night, which seemed to him the longest he had ever known. In spite of his weariness, the howling of the wolves kept him awake, and even when at last the day broke, he was not much better off, for the falling snow had covered up every path, and he did not know which way to turn.

At length he made out some sort of track, and, though at the beginning it was so rough and slippery that he fell down more than once, it presently became easier and led him into an avenue of trees which ended in a splendid castle.

It seemed to the merchant very strange that no snow had fallen in the avenue, which was entirely composed of orange trees covered with flowers and fruit. When he reached the first court of the castle, he saw before him a flight of agate steps; he went up them and passed through several splendidly furnished rooms. The pleasant warmth of the air revived him, and he felt very hungry, but there seemed to be nobody in all this vast and splendid palace whom he could ask to give him something to eat. Deep silence reigned everywhere. At last, tired of roaming through empty rooms and galleries, he stopped in a room smaller than the rest, where a clear fire was burning and a couch was drawn up cozily close to it. Thinking that this must be prepared for someone who was expected, he sat down to wait till this person should come, and then very soon fell into a sweet sleep.

When his extreme hunger wakened him after several hours, he was still alone, but a little table, upon which was a good dinner, had been drawn up close to him. As he had eaten nothing for twenty-four hours, he lost no time in beginning his meal, hoping that he might soon have an opportunity of thanking his considerate host, whoever it might be. But no one appeared, and even after another long sleep, from which he awoke completely refreshed, there was no sign of anybody, though a fresh meal of dainty cakes and fruit was prepared upon the little table at his elbow. Being naturally timid, he was terrified by the silence, and he resolved to search once more through all the rooms. But it was of no use. Not even a servant was to be seen. There was no sign of life in the palace!

He began to wonder what he should do, and he amused himself by pretending that all the treasures he saw were his own and considering how he would divide them among his children. Then he went down into the garden, and though it was winter everywhere else, here the sun shone, and the birds sang, and the flowers bloomed, and the air was soft and sweet. The merchant, in ecstasy with all he saw and heard, said to himself:

"All this must be meant for me. I will go this minute and bring my children to share all these delights."

In spite of being so cold and weary when he reached the castle, he had taken his horse to the stable and fed it. Now he thought he would saddle it for his homeward journey, and he turned down the path which led to the stable. This path had a hedge of roses on each side of it, and the merchant thought he had never seen or smelt such exquisite flowers. They reminded him of his promise to Beauty, and he stopped and had just gathered one to take to her when he was startled by a strange noise behind him. Turning round, he saw a frightful Beast, which seemed to be very angry and said in a terrible voice:

"Who told you that you might gather my roses? Was it not enough that I allowed you to be in my palace and was kind to you? This is the way you show your gratitude, by stealing my flowers! But your insolence shall not go unpunished."

The merchant, terrified by these furious words, dropped the fatal rose and, throwing himself on his knees, cried out:

"Pardon me, noble sir. I am truly grateful to you for your hospitality, which was so magnificent that I could not imagine that you would be offended by my taking such a little thing as a rose."

But the Beast's anger was not lessened by this speech.

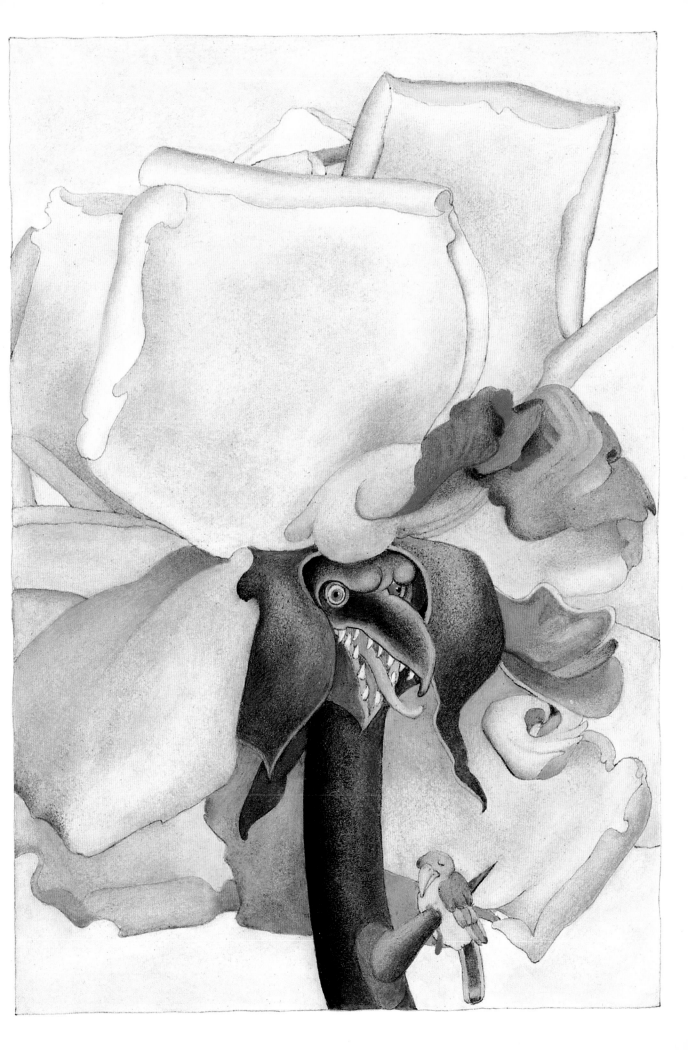

"You are very ready with excuses and flattery," he cried, "but that will not save you from the death you deserve."

"Alas!" thought the merchant, "if my daughter Beauty could only know what danger her rose has brought me!"

And in despair he began to tell the Beast all his misfortunes and the reason for his journey, not forgetting to mention Beauty's request.

"A king's ransom would hardly have procured all that my other daughters asked," he said, "but I thought that I might at least take Beauty her rose. I beg you to forgive me, for you see I meant no harm."

The Beast considered for a moment, and then he said, in a less furious tone:

"I will forgive you on one condition—that is, that you will give me one of your daughters."

"Ah!" cried the merchant. "If I were cruel enough to buy my own life at the expense of one of my children's, what excuse could I invent to bring her here?"

"No excuse would be necessary," answered the Beast. "If she comes at all, she must come willingly. On no other condition will I have her. See if any one of them is courageous enough and loves you well enough to come and save your life. You seem to be an honest man, so I will trust you to go home. I give you a month to see if one of your daughters will come back with you and stay here, to let you go free. If none of them is willing, you must come alone, after bidding them good-bye forever, for then you will belong to me. And do not imagine you can hide from me, for if you fail to keep your word, I will come and fetch you!" added the Beast grimly.

The merchant accepted this proposal, though he did not really think any of his daughters would be persuaded to come. He promised to return at the time appointed, and then, anxious to escape from the presence of the Beast, he asked permission to set off at once. But the Beast answered that he could not go until the next day.

"Then you will find a horse ready for you," he said. "Now go and eat your supper and await my orders."

The poor merchant, more dead than alive, went back to his room where the most delicious supper was already served on the little table which was drawn up before a blazing fire. But he was too terrified to eat and only tasted a few of the dishes, for fear the Beast should be angry if he did not obey his orders. When he had finished, he heard a great noise in the next room, which he knew meant that the Beast was coming. As he could do nothing to escape the Beast's visit, the only thing that remained was to seem as little afraid as possible. When the Beast appeared and asked roughly if he had supped well, the merchant answered humbly that he had, thanks to his host's kindness. Then the Beast warned him to remember their agreement and to prepare his daughter exactly for what she had to expect.

"Do not get up tomorrow," he added, "until you see the sun and hear a golden bell ring. Then you will find your breakfast waiting for you here, and the horse you are to ride will be ready in the courtyard. He will also bring you back again when you come with your daughter a month hence. Farewell. Take a rose to Beauty, and remember your promise!"

The merchant was only too glad when the Beast went away, and though he could not sleep for sadness, he lay down until the sun rose. Then, after a hasty breakfast, he went to gather Beauty's rose and mounted his horse, which carried him off so swiftly that in an instant he had lost sight of the palace, and he was still wrapped in gloomy thoughts when it stopped before the door of the cottage.

His sons and daughters, who had been very uneasy at his long absence, rushed to meet him, eager to know the result of his journey, which, seeing him mounted upon a splendid horse and wrapped in a rich mantle, they supposed was favorable. He hid the truth from them at first, only saying sadly to Beauty as he gave her the rose:

"Here is what you asked me to bring; you little know what it has cost."

But this excited their curiosity so greatly that presently he told them his adventures beginning to end, and then they were all very unhappy. The girls lamented loudly over their lost hopes, and the sons declared that their father should not return to this terrible castle and began to make plans for killing the Beast if it should come to fetch him. But he reminded them that he had promised to go back. Then the girls were very angry with Beauty and said it was all her fault: if she had asked for something sensible this would never have happened. They complained bitterly that they should have to suffer for her folly.

Poor Beauty, much distressed, said to them:

"I have indeed caused this misfortune, but I assure you I did it innocently. Who could have guessed that to ask for a rose in the middle of summer would cause so much misery? But as I did the mischief, it is only just that I should suffer for it. I will therefore go back with my father to keep his promise."

At first nobody would hear of this arrangement, and her father and brothers, who loved her dearly, declared that nothing should make them let her go. But Beauty was firm. As the time drew near she divided all her little possessions between her sisters and said goodbye to everything she loved. When the fatal day came, she encouraged and cheered her father as they mounted the horse which had brought him back. It

seemed to fly rather than gallop, but so smoothly that Beauty was not frightened; indeed, she would have enjoyed the journey if she had not feared what might happen to her at the end of it. Her father still tried to persuade her to go back, but in vain. While they were talking the night fell, and then, to their great surprise, wonderful colored lights began to shine in all directions, and splendid fireworks blazed out before them. All the forest was illuminated by them, and it even felt pleasantly warm, though the forest had been bitterly cold before. This lasted until they reached the avenue of orange trees, where statues were holding flaming torches. When they got nearer to the palace, they saw that it was illuminated from the roof to the ground, and music sounded softly from the courtyard. "The Beast must be very hungry," said

Beauty, trying to laugh, "if he makes all this rejoicing over the arrival of his prey."

But in spite of her anxiety, she could not help admiring all the wonderful things she saw.

The horse stopped at the foot of the flight of steps leading to the terrace, and when they dismounted, her father led her to the little room he had been in before, where they found a splendid fire burning, and the table daintily spread with a delicious supper.

The merchant knew that this was meant for them. Beauty, who was rather less frightened now that she had passed through so many rooms and had seen nothing of the Beast, was quite willing to begin, for her long ride had made her very hungry. They had hardly finished their meal when the noise of the Beast's footsteps was heard approaching, and Beauty clung to her father in terror, which became all the greater when she saw how frightened he was. But when the Beast really appeared, though she trembled at the sight of him, she made a great effort to hide her horror and saluted him respectfully.

This evidently pleased the Beast. After looking at her he said, in a tone that might have struck terror into the boldest heart, though he did not seem to be angry:

"Good evening, old man. Good evening, Beauty."

The merchant was too terrified to reply, but Beauty answered sweetly:

"Good evening, Beast."

"Have you come willingly?" asked the Beast. "Will you be content to stay here when your father goes away?"

Beauty answered bravely that she was quite prepared to stay.

"I am pleased with you," said the Beast. "As you have come of your own accord, you may stay. As for you, old man," he added, turning to the merchant, "at sunrise tomorrow you will take your departure. When the bell rings get up quickly and eat your breakfast, and you will find the same horse waiting to take you home. But remember that you must never expect to see my palace again."

Then turning to Beauty, he said:

"Take your father into the next room and help him choose everything you think your brothers and sisters would like to have. You will find two traveling trunks there; fill them as full as you can. It is only fair that you should send them something very precious as a remembrance of yourself."

Then he went away, after saying

"Good-bye, Beauty; good-bye, old man"; and though Beauty was beginning to think with great dismay of her father's departure, she was afraid to disobey the Beast's orders, and they went into the next room, which had shelves and cupboards all around it. They were greatly surprised at the riches it contained. There were splendid dresses fit for a queen, with all the ornaments that were to be worn with them. When Beauty opened the cupboards, she was quite dazzled by the gorgeous jewels that lay in heaps upon every shelf. After choosing a vast quantity, which she divided between her sisters—for she had made a heap of the wonderful dresses for each of them—she opened the last chest which was full of gold.

"I think, Father," she said, "that as the gold will be more useful to you, we

had better take out the other things and fill the trunks with it."

So they did this, but the more they put in, the more room there seemed to be. At last they put back all the jewels and dresses they had taken out, and Beauty even added as many more of the jewels as she could carry at once. Then the trunks still were not too full, but they were so heavy that an elephant could not have carried them!

"The Beast was mocking us," cried the merchant. "He must have pretended to give us all these things, knowing that I could not carry them away."

"Let us wait and see," said Beauty. "I cannot believe that he meant to deceive us. All we can do is to fasten them up and leave them ready."

So they did this and returned to the little room, where to their astonish-ment, they found breakfast ready. The merchant ate his with a good appetite, as the Beast's generosity made him believe that he might perhaps venture to come back soon and see Beauty. But she felt sure that her father was leaving her forever, so she was very sad when the bell rang sharply for the second time and warned them that the time had come to part. They went down into the courtyard where two horses were wait-ing, one loaded with the two trunks and the other for him to ride. They were pawing the ground in their impa-tience to start, and the merchant was forced to bid Beauty a hasty farewell. As soon as her father mounted his horse, he went off at such a pace that Beauty lost sight of him in an instant. Then she began to cry and wandered sadly back to her own room.

But she soon found that she was very sleepy, and because she had nothing better to do, she lay down and instantly fell asleep. She then dreamed that she was walking by a brook bordered with trees, and lamenting her sad fate, when a young prince, handsomer than anyone she had ever seen, and with a voice that went straight to her heart, came and said to her, "Ah, Beauty! You are not so unfortunate as you suppose. Here you will be rewarded for all you have suffered elsewhere. Your every wish shall be gratified. Only try to find me out, no matter how I may be disguised, as I love you dearly. In making me happy you will find your own happiness. Be as true hearted as you are beautiful, and we shall have nothing left to wish for."

"What can I do, Prince, to make you happy?" asked Beauty.

"Only be grateful," he answered, "and do not trust too much to your eyes. But above all, do not desert me until you have saved me from my cruel misery."

After this she dreamed she found herself in a room with a stately and beautiful lady who said to her:

"Dear Beauty, try not to miss all you have left behind you, for you are destined to a better fate. Only do not let yourself be deceived by appearances."

Beauty found her dreams so interesting that she was in no hurry to awake, but presently the clock roused her by calling her name softly twelve times. Then she got up and found her dressing table set out with everything she could possibly want. When her grooming was finished, she found dinner was waiting in the room next to hers.

But dinner does not take very long when you are all by yourself and very soon she sat down cozily in the corner of a sofa, and began to think about the charming Prince she had seen in her dream.

"He said I could make him happy," said Beauty to herself.

"It seems, then, that this horrible Beast keeps him a prisoner. How can I set him free? I wonder why they both told me not to trust appearances? I don't understand it. But, after all, it was only a dream, so why should I trouble myself about it? I had better go and find something to do to amuse myself."

So she got up and began to explore some of the many rooms of the palace.

The first she entered was lined with mirrors, and Beauty saw herself reflected on every side, and thought she had never seen such a charming room. Then a bracelet which was hanging from a chandelier caught her eye, and on taking it down she was greatly surprised to find that it held a portrait of her unknown admirer, just as she had seen him in her dream. With great delight she slipped the bracelet on her arm and went into a gallery of pictures, where she soon found a portrait of the same handsome Prince, as large as life, and so well painted that as she studied it he seemed to smile kindly at her. Tearing herself away from the portrait at last, she passed through into a room which contained every musical instrument under the sun. Here she amused herself for a long while in trying some of the instruments and singing until she was tired. The next room was a

library, and she saw everything she had ever wanted to read, as well as everything she had read, and it seemed to her that a whole lifetime would not be enough even to read the names of the books, there were so many. By this time it was growing dusk, and wax candles in diamond and ruby candlesticks were beginning to light themselves in every room.

Beauty found her supper served just at the time she preferred to have it, but she did not see anyone or hear a sound, and though her father had warned her that she would be alone, she began to find it rather dull.

But she heard the Beast coming and wondered tremblingly if he meant to eat her up now.

However, he did not seem at all ferocious, and only said gruffly:

"Good evening, Beauty."

She answered cheerfully and managed to conceal her terror. Then the Beast asked her how she had been amusing herself, and she told him all the rooms she had seen.

Then he asked if she thought she could be happy in his palace, and Beauty answered that everything was so beautiful that she would be very hard to please if she could not be happy. After about an hour's talk, Beauty began to think that the Beast was not nearly so terrible as she had supposed at first. Then he got up to leave her and said in his gruff voice:

"Do you love me, Beauty? Will you marry me?"

"Oh! What shall I say?" cried Beauty, for she was afraid to make the Beast angry by refusing.

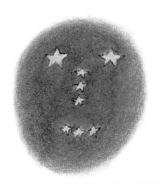

"Say 'yes' or 'no' without fear," he replied.

"Oh! No, Beast," said Beauty hastily.

"Since you will not, then good night, Beauty," he said.

And she answered, "Good night, Beast," very glad to find that her refusal had not provoked him. And after he was gone she was very soon in bed and asleep, dreaming of her unknown Prince. She thought he came and said to her:

"Ah, Beauty! Why are you so unkind to me? I fear I am fated to be unhappy for many a long day still."

And then her dreams changed, but the charming Prince figured in them all. When morning came, her first thought was to look at the portrait and see if it was really like him, and she found that it certainly was.

This morning she decided to amuse herself in the garden, for the sun shone and all the fountains were flowing. She was astonished to find the very place was familiar to her, and she came to the brook where the myrtle trees were growing, where she had first met the Prince in her dream. That made her think more than ever that he must be kept a prisoner by the Beast. When she was tired, she went back to the palace and found a new room full of material for every kind of work—ribbons to make into bows and silks to work into flowers. Then there was an aviary full of rare birds, which were so tame that they flew to Beauty as soon as they saw her and perched upon her shoulders and her head.

"Pretty little creatures," she said, "how I wish that your cage was nearer to my room, that I might often hear you sing!"

Upon saying that, Beauty opened a door and found to her delight that it led into her own room, though she had thought it was quite the other side of the palace.

There were more birds in a room farther on, with parrots and cockatoos that could talk, and they greeted Beauty by name. Indeed, she found them so entertaining that she took one or two back to her room, and they talked to her while she was at supper, after which the Beast paid her his usual visit. He asked the same question as before, and then with a gruff "good night" he took his departure, and Beauty went to bed to dream of her mysterious Prince.

The days passed swiftly in different amusements, and after a while Beauty found another strange thing in the palace, which often pleased her when she was tired of being alone. There was one room which she had not noticed particularly; it was empty, except that under each of the windows stood a very comfortable chair. The first time she had looked out of the window it had seemed to her that a black curtain prevented her from seeing anything outside. But the second time she went into the room, happening to be tired, she sat down in one of the chairs. Instantly the curtain was rolled aside, and a most amusing pantomime was acted before her. There were dances, colored lights, music, and pretty dresses; it was all so gay that Beauty was in ecstasy. After that she tried the other seven windows in turn, and there was some new and surprising entertainment to be seen from each of them, so that Beauty never could feel lonely anymore. Every evening after supper the Beast came to see her, and always before saying good night asked her in his terrible voice:

"Beauty, will you marry me?"

And it seemed to Beauty, now that she understood him better, that when she said, "No, Beast," he went away quite sad. But her happy dreams of the handsome young Prince soon made her forget the poor Beast, and the only thing that at all disturbed her was to be constantly told to distrust appearances, to let her heart guide her, and not let her eyes guide her, and many other equally perplexing things, which, consider as she would, she could not understand.

So everything went on for a long time, until at last, happy as she was, Beauty began to long for the sight of her father and her brothers and sisters. One night, seeing her look very sad, the Beast asked her what was the matter. Beauty had quite ceased to be afraid of him. Now she knew that he was really gentle despite his ferocious looks and his dreadful voice. So she answered that she was longing to see her home once more. Upon hearing this, the Beast seemed deadly distressed and cried miserably.

"Ah! Beauty, have you the heart to desert an unhappy Beast like this? What more do you want to make you happy? Is it because you hate me that you want to escape?"

"No, dear Beast," answered Beauty softly. "I do not hate you, and I should be very sorry never to see you anymore, but I long to see my father again. Only let me go for two months, and I promise to come back to you and stay for the rest of my life."

The Beast, who had been sighing dolefully while she spoke, now replied:

"I cannot refuse anything you ask, even though it could cost me my life. Take the four boxes you will find in the room next to your own and fill them with everything you wish to take with you. But remember your promise and come back when the two months are over, or you may have cause to repent it, for if you do not arrive in good time, you will find your faithful Beast dead. You will not need any chariot to bring you back. Only say good-bye to all your brothers and sisters the night before you leave. When you have gone to bed, turn this ring round upon your finger and say firmly: 'I wish to go

back to my palace and see my Beast again.' Good night, Beauty. Fear nothing, sleep peacefully, and before long you shall see your father once more."

As soon as Beauty was alone she hastened to fill the boxes with all the rare and precious things she saw around her. Only when she was tired of heaping things into them did the boxes seem to be full.

Then she went to bed, but could hardly sleep for joy. And when at last she did begin to dream of her beloved Prince, she was grieved to see him stretched upon a grassy bank sad and weary, hardly like himself.

"What is the matter?" she cried.

But he looked reproachfully at her and said, "How can you ask me, cruel one? Are you not leaving me to my death perhaps?"

"Ah! Don't be so sorrowful," cried Beauty. "I am only going to assure my father that I am safe and happy. I have promised the Beast faithfully that I will come back, and he would die of grief if I did not keep my word!"

"What would that matter to you?" said the Prince. "Surely you would not care?"

"Indeed I should be ungrateful if I did not care for such a kind Beast," cried Beauty indignantly. "I would die to save him from pain. I assure you it is not his fault that he is so ugly."

Just then a strange sound woke her—someone was speaking not very far away. Opening her eyes, she found herself in a room she had never seen before, which was certainly not nearly so splendid as those she was used to in the Beast's palace. Where could she be?

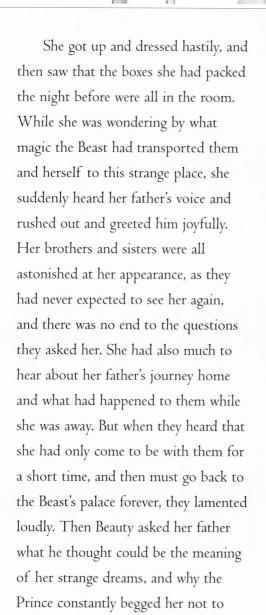

She got up and dressed hastily, and then saw that the boxes she had packed the night before were all in the room. While she was wondering by what magic the Beast had transported them and herself to this strange place, she suddenly heard her father's voice and rushed out and greeted him joyfully. Her brothers and sisters were all astonished at her appearance, as they had never expected to see her again, and there was no end to the questions they asked her. She had also much to hear about her father's journey home and what had happened to them while she was away. But when they heard that she had only come to be with them for a short time, and then must go back to the Beast's palace forever, they lamented loudly. Then Beauty asked her father what he thought could be the meaning of her strange dreams, and why the Prince constantly begged her not to

trust appearances. After much consideration he answered:

"You tell me yourself that the Beast, frightful as he is, loves you dearly, and deserves your love and gratitude for his gentleness and kindness. I think the Prince must mean for you to understand that you ought to reward him by doing as he wishes you to, in spite of his ugliness."

Beauty could not help seeing that this seemed very probable. Still, when she thought of her dear Prince who was so handsome, she did not feel at all inclined to marry the Beast. At any rate, for two months she need not decide, but could enjoy herself with her sisters. Though they were rich now and lived in a town again, with plenty of acquaintances, Beauty found that nothing amused her very much. She often thought of the palace, where she was so happy. At home she never once dreamed

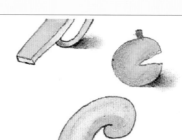

of her dear Prince, and she felt quite sad without him.

Then her sisters seemed to have become quite used to being without her, and they even found her in the way, so Beauty felt she would not be sorry when the two months were over. But her father and brothers begged her to stay and seemed so grieved at the thought of her departure, that she did not have the courage to say good-bye to them. Every day when she got up she meant to say it at night, and when night came she put if off again, until at last she had a dismal dream which helped her to make up her mind. She thought she was wandering on a lonely path in the palace gardens, when she heard groans which seemed to come from some bushes hiding the entrance of a cave, and running quickly to see what could be the matter, she found the Beast stretched out upon his side,

apparently dying. He reproached her faintly for being the cause of his distress. At the same moment, a stately lady appeared and said very gravely:

"Ah! Beauty, you are only just in time to save his life. See what happens when people do not keep their promises! If you had delayed one day more, you would have found him dead."

Beauty was so terrified by this dream that the next morning she announced her intention of going back at once, and that very night she said good-bye to her father and all her brothers and sisters. As soon as she was in bed, she turned her ring round upon her finger and said firmly:

"I wish to go back to my palace and see my Beast again," as she had been told to do.

Then she fell asleep instantly and woke up to hear the clock saying, "Beauty, Beauty," twelve times in its musical voice, which told her at once that she was really in the palace once more. Everything was just as before, and her birds were so glad to see her! But Beauty thought she had never known such a long day, for she was so anxious to see the Beast again that she felt as if supper time should never come.

But when it did come and no Beast appeared, she was really frightened. After listening and waiting for a long time, she ran down into the garden to search for him. Up and down the paths and avenues ran poor Beauty, calling him in vain, for no one answered and not a trace of him could she find, until at last, quite tired, she stopped for a minute's rest and saw that she was standing opposite the shady path she had seen in her dream. She rushed down it, and, sure enough, there was the cave and in it lay the Beast—asleep, as Beauty thought. Quite glad to have found him, she ran up and stroked his head, but to her horror he did not move or open his eyes.

"Oh! He is dead, and it is all my fault," said Beauty, crying bitterly.

But then, looking at him again, she fancied he still breathed. Hastily fetching some water from the nearest fountain, she sprinkled it over his face, and to her great delight he began to revive.

"Oh! Beast, how you frightened me!" she cried. "I never knew how much I loved you until just now, when I feared I was too late to save your life."

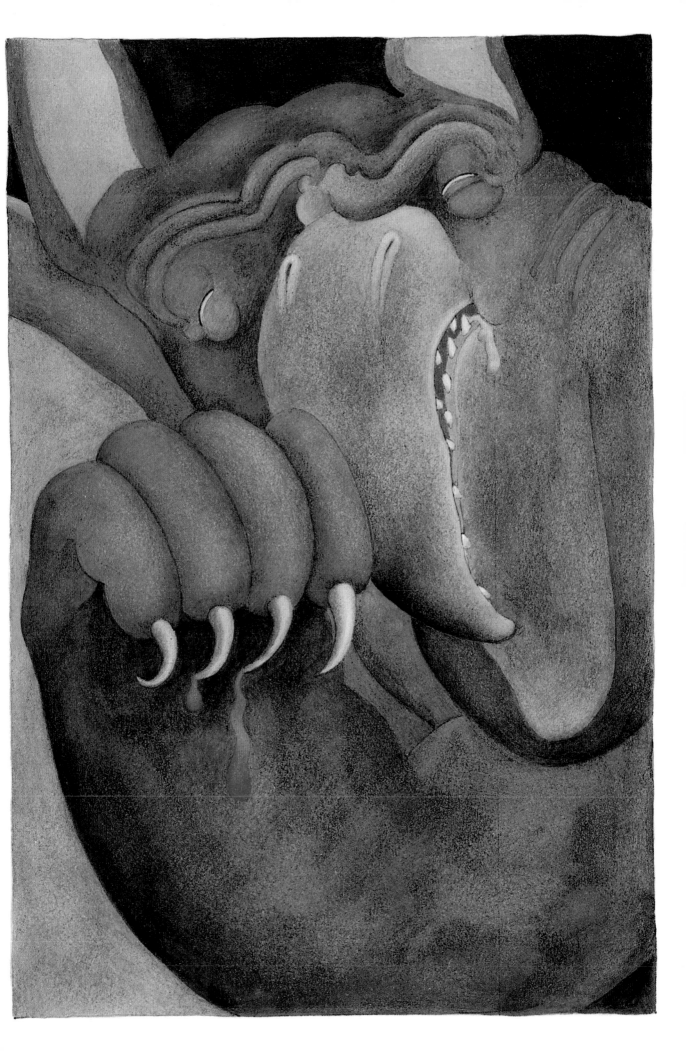

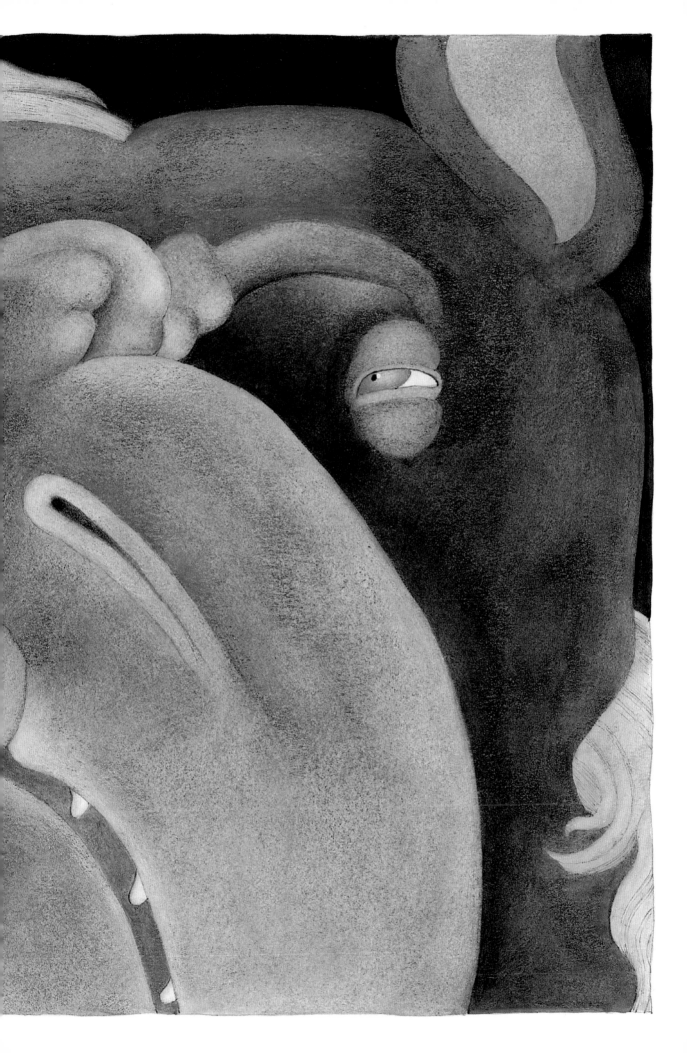

"Can you really love such an ugly creature as I am?" asked the Beast faintly. "Ah! Beauty, you came just in time. I was dying because I thought you had forgotten your promise. But go back now and rest, I shall see you again by and by."

Beauty, who had half expected that he would be angry with her, was reassured by his gentle voice and went back to the palace, where supper was awaiting her. Afterwards the Beast came in as usual and talked about the time she had spent with her father, asking if she had enjoyed herself and if they all had been very glad to see her.

Beauty answered politely and quite enjoyed telling him all that had happened to her. And when at last the time came for him to go, he asked the question that he had so often asked before:

"Beauty, will you marry me?"

She answered softly, "Yes, dear Beast."

As she spoke, a blaze of light sprang up before the windows of the palace, fireworks crackled and guns banged. Across the avenue of orange trees, in letters all made of fireflies, was written: "Long live the Prince and his beautiful bride."

Turning to ask the Beast what it could all mean, Beauty found that he had disappeared, and in his place stood her long-loved Prince! At the same moment the heels of a chariot were heard upon the terrace, and two ladies entered the room. One of them Beauty recognized as the stately lady she had seen in her dreams; the other was also so grand and queenly that Beauty hardly knew which to greet first.

But the one she already knew said to her companion:

"Well, Queen, this is Beauty, who has had the courage to rescue your son from the terrible enchantment. They love one another, and only your consent to their marriage is needed to make them perfectly happy."

"I consent with all my heart," cried the Queen. "How can I ever thank you enough, charming girl, for having restored my dear son to his natural form?"

And then she tenderly embraced Beauty and the Prince, who had meanwhile been greeting the Fairy and receiving her congratulations.

"Now," said the Fairy to Beauty, "I suppose you would like me to send for all your brothers and sisters to dance at your wedding?"

And so she did, and the marriage was celebrated the very next day with the utmost splendor, and Beauty and the Prince lived happily ever after.

CINDERELLA

CHARLES PERRAULT

ILLUSTRATED BY ROBERTO INNOCENTI

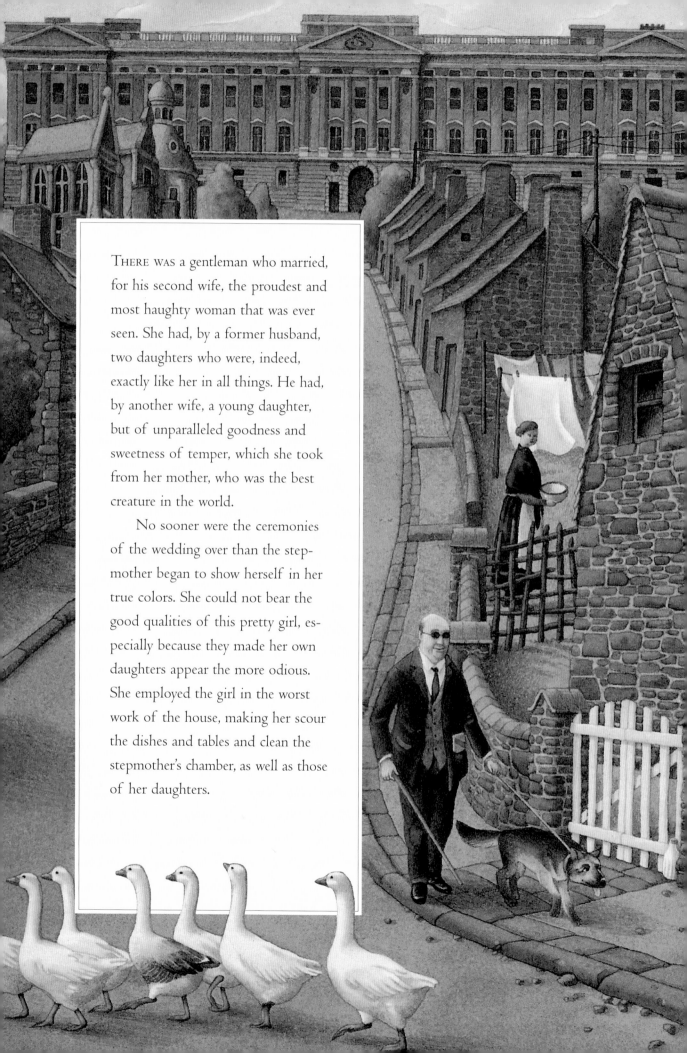

There was a gentleman who married, for his second wife, the proudest and most haughty woman that was ever seen. She had, by a former husband, two daughters who were, indeed, exactly like her in all things. He had, by another wife, a young daughter, but of unparalleled goodness and sweetness of temper, which she took from her mother, who was the best creature in the world.

No sooner were the ceremonies of the wedding over than the step-mother began to show herself in her true colors. She could not bear the good qualities of this pretty girl, especially because they made her own daughters appear the more odious. She employed the girl in the worst work of the house, making her scour the dishes and tables and clean the stepmother's chamber, as well as those of her daughters.

The girl lay up in a sorry attic upon a wretched straw bed, while her stepsisters lay in fine rooms, with floors all inlaid, upon beds of the very newest fashion, and where they had mirrors so large that they might see themselves at their full length from head to foot.

The poor girl bore all patiently and dared not tell her father, who would not have listened for his wife governed him entirely. When the girl had done her work, she used to go into the chimney corner and sit down among cinders and ashes, which made her commonly be called *Cinderwench;* but the youngest stepsister, who was not so rude and uncivil as the eldest, called her Cinderella.

However, Cinderella, notwithstanding her shabby clothes, was a hundred times prettier than her stepsisters, though they were always dressed very richly.

One day it happened that the King's son gave a ball and invited all persons of fashion to it. Our young misses were also invited, for they cut a very grand figure in high society. They were delighted at this invitation and were wonderfully busy in choosing such gowns, petticoats, and headdresses as might become them. This was a new trouble to Cinderella, for it was she who ironed her sisters' linen and plaited their ruffles. They talked all day long of nothing but how they should be dressed.

"For my part," said the eldest, "I will wear my red velvet suit with French trimming."

"And I," said the youngest, "shall have my usual petticoat. But then, to make amends for that, I will put on my gold-flowered gown and my diamond stomacher, which is far from being the most ordinary one in the world."

They sent for the best designer they could get to make up their head-dresses and adjust their hats, and they had their red feathers and patches from Mademoiselle de la Poche.

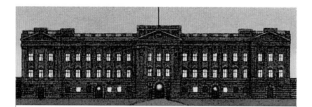

Cinderella was consulted in all these matters, for she had excellent taste. She advised them always for the best and offered her services to style their hair, which they were very willing to have her do.

As she was doing this, they said to her:

"Cinderella, would you not be glad to go to the ball?"

"Alas!" said she. "You only tease me; girls such as I are not suited for balls."

"You are right," they replied. "It would make the people laugh to see a Cinderwench at a ball."

Anyone but Cinderella would have styled their hair awry, but she was very good and dressed them perfectly well. The sisters went almost two days without eating, they were so overcome with joy. They broke more than a dozen laces in trying to be laced up tightly, that they might have a fine slender shape, and they were continually at their mirrors.

At last the happy day came; they went to Court, and Cinderella followed them with longing eyes. When she had lost sight of them, she began weeping.

Her godmother, who saw her all in tears, asked her what was the matter.

"I wish I could, I wish I could—" she was not able to speak the rest, being interrupted by her tears and sobbing.

This godmother of hers, who was a fairy, said to her, "You wish you could go to the ball. Is it not so?"

"Y—es," cried Cinderella, with a great sigh.

"Well," said her godmother, "be but a good girl, and I will arrange that you shall go." Then she took Cinderella into her chamber and said to her, "Run into the garden and bring me a pumpkin."

Cinderella went immediately to gather the finest she could get and brought it to her godmother, not being able to imagine how this pumpkin could make her go to the ball. Her godmother scooped out all the inside of it, leaving nothing but the rind; then she struck it with her wand, and the pumpkin was instantly turned into a fine coach, gilded with gold.

She then went to look into her mousetrap, where she found six mice, all alive, and ordered Cinderella to lift up the trapdoor a little. Then, giving each mouse, as it went out, a little tap with her wand, the mouse was that moment turned into a fine horse, which altogether made a very fine set of six horses of a beautiful mouse-colored dapple-grey. Needing yet a coachman, Cinderella said,

"I will go and see if there is a rat in the rattrap—perhaps we can make a coachman of him."

"You are right," replied her godmother, "go and look."

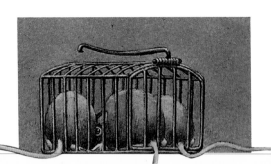

Cinderella brought the trap to her, and in it there were three huge rats. The fairy chose the one with the largest beard, and, having touched him with her wand, he was turned into a fat, jolly coachman who had the sharpest mustache eyes ever beheld. After that, she said to Cinderella:

"Go again into the garden, and you will find six lizards behind the watering pot. Bring them to me."

Cinderella had no sooner done so than her godmother turned them into six footmen who skipped up immediately behind the coach. Their uniforms were all decorated with gold and silver, and they clung as close behind each other as if they had done nothing else their whole lives. The fairy then said to Cinderella:

"You see here a coach fit to go to the ball. Are you not pleased with it?"

"Oh! Yes," cried she. "But must I go as I am, in these nasty rags?"

Her godmother touched her with her wand, and, at the same instant, her clothes were turned into cloth of gold and silver, all beset with jewels. This done, she gave her a pair of glass slippers, the prettiest in the whole world. Being thus decked out, she got up into her coach. But her godmother, above all things, commanded her not to stay till after midnight, telling her, at the same time, that if she stayed one moment longer, the coach would be a pumpkin again, her horses mice, her coachman a rat, her footmen lizards, and her clothes would become just as they were before.

Cinderella promised her godmother she would not fail to leave the ball before midnight. Then away she drove, scarce able to contain herself for joy.

The King's son, who was told that
a great princess, whom nobody knew,
had come, ran out to receive her. He
gave her his hand as she alighted from
the coach and led her into the hall,
among all the company. There was
immediately a profound silence; they
stopped dancing and the violins ceased
to play, so attentive was everyone to
contemplate the singular beauties of
the unknown newcomer. Nothing was
then heard but a confused noise of:

"Ha! How beautiful she is!"

The King himself, old as he was,
could not help watching her and telling
the Queen that it was a long time since
he had seen so beautiful and lovely a
creature.

All the ladies were busied in considering her clothes and headdress, that they might have some made after the same pattern, provided they could find such wonderful materials and as able hands to make them.

The King's son led Cinderella to the most honorable seat and afterwards took her out to dance with him. She danced so very gracefully that they all the more admired her. A fine meal was served, but the young prince ate not a morsel, so intently was he gazing upon her.

She went and sat down by her stepsisters, showing them great kindness, giving them part of the oranges and citrons which the Prince had given her, which very much surprised them, for they did not know her. While Cinderella was thus amusing her stepsisters, she heard the clock strike eleven and three-quarters, whereupon she immediately excused herself from the company and hurried away as fast as she could.

When she got home, she ran to seek out her godmother, and, after having thanked her, she said she could not but heartily wish that she might go the next day to the ball, because the King's son had invited her.

As she was eagerly telling her godmother what had passed at the ball, her two stepsisters knocked at the door, which Cinderella ran and opened.

"How long you have stayed!" cried she, gaping, rubbing her eyes and stretching herself as if she had been just awakened from sleep. She had not, of course, slept since they left.

"If you had been at the ball," said one of her stepsisters, "you would not have been tired with it. There came the finest princess, the most beautiful ever seen with mortal eyes. She showed us great kindness and gave us oranges and citrons."

Cinderella seemed very indifferent in the matter. Indeed, she asked them the name of the princess, but they told her they did not know it, and that the King's son was very taken with her and would give all the world to know who she was. At this, Cinderella smiled and replied:

"She must, then, be very beautiful indeed. How happy you have been! Could I see her? Ah! dear Miss Charlotte, do lend me your yellow suit of clothes which you wear every day."

"Ay, to be sure!" cried Miss Charlotte. "Lend my clothes to such a dirty Cinderwench as you are! I should be a fool."

Cinderella, indeed, well expected such an answer and was very glad of the refusal, for she would have been embarrassed if her stepsister had lent her what she asked for in jest.

The next day, the two sisters were at the ball and so was Cinderella, but dressed more magnificently than before. The King's son was always by her side and never ceased his compliments and kind speeches to her. She quite forgot what her godmother had told her; so that she, at last, counted the clock striking twelve when she thought it was no more than eleven. She then rose up and fled, as nimble as a deer. The Prince followed but could not overtake her. She left behind one of her glass slippers, which the Prince picked up most carefully. She got home, but quite out of breath and in her nasty old clothes, having nothing left of all her finery but one of the little slippers, matching the one she dropped. The guards at the palace gate were asked if they had seen a princess leave the palace grounds.

They had seen nobody go out but a young girl, very poorly dressed, who had more the air of a poor country wench than a gentlewoman.

When the two sisters returned from the ball, Cinderella asked them if they had been well entertained and if the fine lady had been there.

They told her yes, but that she hurried away immediately when it struck twelve, and with so much haste that she dropped one of her little glass slippers, the prettiest in the world, which the King's son had picked up; that he had done nothing but look at her all the time at the ball. Most certainly he was very much in love with the beautiful girl who owned the glass slipper.

What they said was very true.
For a few days after, the King's son
proclaimed, by sound of trumpet,
that he would marry her whose foot
this slipper would just fit. His
stewards began to try it upon the
princesses, then the duchesses and
all the Court, but in vain. It was also
brought to the two sisters, who did
all they possibly could to thrust
their foot into the slipper, but to
no avail.

Cinderella, who saw all this and knew her slipper, said to them, laughing:

"Let me see if it will not fit me."

Her sisters burst out laughing and began to ridicule her. The gentleman who was sent to try the slipper looked earnestly at Cinderella, and, finding her very pretty, said it was only fair that she should try and that he had orders to let everyone try to put the slipper on.

He asked Cinderella to sit down, and, putting the slipper to her foot, he found it went on very easily and fit her as if it had been made of wax. The astonishment her two sisters felt was excessively great, but it became even greater when Cinderella pulled out of her pocket the other slipper and put it on her foot.

Thereupon, in came her god-mother, who touched Cinderella's clothes, making them richer and more magnificent than any of those she had worn before.

And now her two sisters found her to be that fine, beautiful lady whom they had seen at the ball. They threw themselves at her feet to beg pardon for all the ill treatment they had heaped upon her. Cinderella helped them up, and, as she embraced them, cried that she forgave them with all her heart and desired them always to love her.

She was led to the young Prince dressed as she was. He thought her more charming than ever, and, a few days after, married her. Cinderella, who was no less good than beautiful, gave her two sisters lodgings in the palace, and that very same day she matched them with two great lords of the Court.

HANSEL & GRETEL

GRIMM

ILLUSTRATED BY MONIQUE FELIX

Once upon a time

THERE DWELT at the edge of a large forest a poor woodcutter with his wife and two children; the boy was called Hansel and the girl Gretel. He had little to live on, and once, when there was a great famine in the land, he couldn't even provide them with daily bread. One night, as he was tossing about in bed, full of worry, he sighed and said to his wife:

"What's to become of us? How are we to support our poor children, now that we have nothing more for ourselves?"

"I'll tell you what, husband," answered the woman who was stepmother to Hansel and Gretel. "Early tomorrow morning we will take the children out into the thickest part of the woods. There we shall light a fire for them and give them each a piece of bread; then we'll go on to our work and leave them alone. They won't be able to find their way home, and we shall thus be rid of them."

"No, wife," said her husband, "that I won't do; how could I find it in my heart to leave my children alone in the woods? The wild beasts would soon come and tear them to pieces."

"Oh! You fool," she said, "then we must all four die of hunger, and you may just as well go and plane the boards for our coffins." And she left him no peace till he consented.

"But I can't help feeling sorry for the poor children," added the husband.

The children, too, had not been able to sleep for hunger, and had heard what their stepmother had said to their father. Gretel wept bitterly and spoke to Hansel. "Now we shall surely die."

"No, no, Gretel," said Hansel, "don't fret. I'll find a way to escape."

And when his father and step-mother had fallen asleep, he got up, slipped on his little coat, opened the back door and stole out. The moon was shining clearly, and the white pebbles which lay in front of the house glittered like bits of silver. Hansel bent down and filled his pocket with as many of them as he could. Then he went back and said to Gretel:

"Be comforted, my dear little sister, and go to sleep. God will not desert us." And he lay down in bed again.

At daybreak, even before the sun was up, the woman came and woke the two children:

"Get up, you lazy-bones, we're all going to the forest to fetch wood."

She gave them each a bit of bread and spoke:

"Here's something for your lunch, but don't eat it up too soon, for it's all you'll get."

Gretel put the bread under her apron, as Hansel had the stones in his pocket. Then they all set out together on the way to the forest.

After they had walked for a while, Hansel stood still and looked back at the house every so often. His father saw him and asked:

"Hansel, what are you gazing at there, and why do you always remain behind? Come along and don't lose your footing."

"Oh! father," said Hansel, "I am looking back at my white kitten, which is sitting on the roof, waving me a farewell."

The woman exclaimed:

"What a donkey you are! That isn't your kitten, that's the morning sun shining on the chimney."

But in fact Hansel had not looked back at his kitten. Rather he had always dropped one of the white pebbles out of his pocket onto the path.

When they had reached the middle of the forest, the father said:

"Now, children, go and fetch a lot of wood, and I'll light a fire so you won't be cold."

Hansel and Gretel heaped up brushwood till they had made a pile nearly the size of a small hill. The brushwood was set afire, and when the flames leaped high the woman said:

"Now lie down next to the fire, children, and rest yourselves. We are going into the forest to cut down wood. When we've finished we'll come back and get you."

Hansel and Gretel sat down beside the fire, and at midday ate their little bits of bread. They heard the strokes of the axe, so they thought their father was quite near. But it was no axe they heard, just a branch he had tied on to a dead tree that was blown about by the wind. After they had waited for a long time, their eyes closed with fatigue and they fell fast asleep.

When they awoke, it was pitch-dark. Gretel began to cry, and said:

"How are we ever going to get out of the woods?"

But Hansel comforted her.

"Wait a bit," he said, "till the moon is up, and then we'll find our way sure enough."

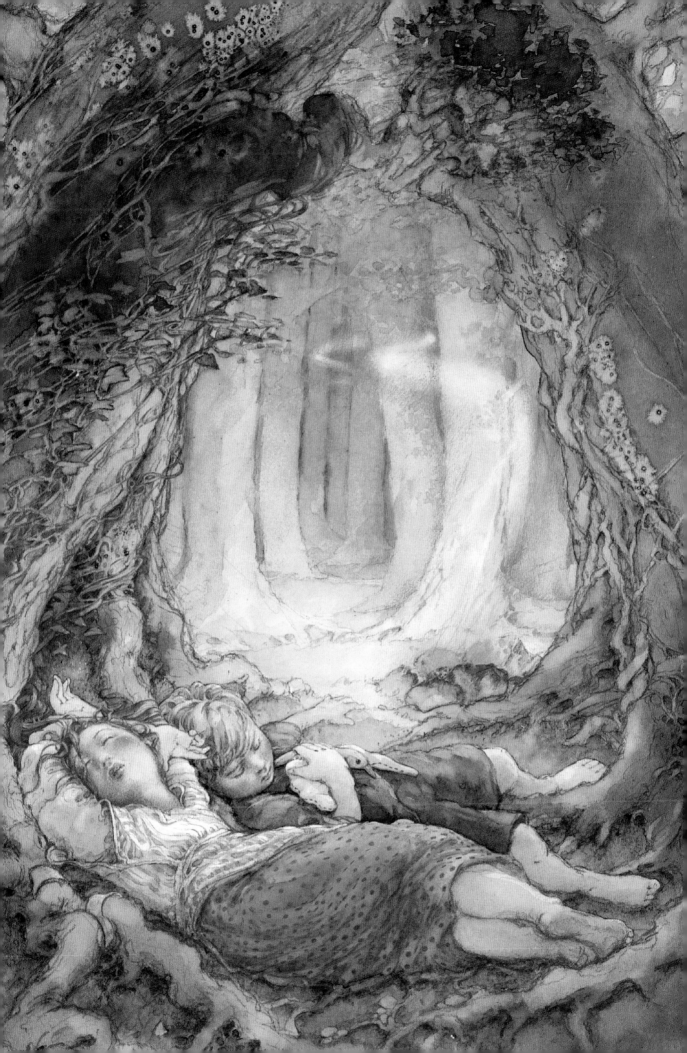

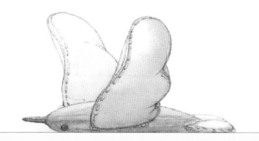

When the full moon had risen, he took his sister by the hand and followed the pebbles, which shone like new pennies and showed them the path. They walked all through the night, and at daybreak reached their father's house. They knocked at the door, and when the woman opened it she exclaimed:

"You naughty children, what a long time you've slept in the woods! We thought you were never going to come back."

But the father rejoiced, for he had felt guilty for leaving his children behind by themselves.

Not long afterwards there was again great famine in the land, and the children heard their stepmother address their father in bed one night:

"Everything is eaten up once more; we have only a half a loaf of bread in the house, and when that's gone we will starve. The children must be gotten rid of. We'll lead them deeper into the woods this time, so that they won't be able to find their way out again. There is no other way to save ourselves."

The man's heart sank at these words, and he thought:

"Surely it would be better to share the last bite of food with one's children!"

But his wife would not listen to his arguments, and did nothing but scold him. If a man yields once, he's done for. And because he had given in to his wife the first time, he was forced to do so the second.

The children were awake and had heard the conversation. When his father and stepmother were asleep, Hansel got up, and wanted to go out and pick up pebbles again, as he had done the first time; but the woman had barred the door, and Hansel couldn't get out. But he consoled his little sister, and said:

"Don't cry, Gretel, and sleep peacefully, for God is sure to help us."

At early dawn the woman came and made the children get up. They received their bit of bread, but it was even smaller than the time before. On the way to the woods, Hansel crumbled it in his pocket, and every few minutes he stood still and dropped a crumb on the ground.

"Hansel, what are you stopping and looking back for?" asked his father.

"I'm looking back at my little pigeon, which is sitting on the roof waving me farewell," answered Hansel.

"Fool!" said the wife, "that isn't your pigeon, it's the morning sun glittering on the chimney."

But Hansel gradually threw all his crumbs onto the path. The woman led the children still deeper into the forest, farther than they had ever been in their lives. Then a big fire was lit again, and the stepmother said:

"Just sit down there, children, and if you're tired you can sleep a bit; we're going into the forest to cut wood, and in the evening when we're finished, we'll come back to get you."

At midday Gretel divided her bread with Hansel, for he had dropped all of his along the path. Then they fell asleep, and evening passed away, but nobody came back for the poor children.

They didn't wake up till it was pitch-dark, and Hansel comforted his sister, saying:

"Just wait, Gretel, till the moon rises, then we shall see the breadcrumbs I scattered along the path; they will show us the way back to the house."

When the moon appeared they got up, but they found no crumbs, for the thousands of birds that fly about the woods and fields had picked them all up.

"Never mind," said Hansel to Gretel. "You'll see we will still find a way out."

They wandered about the whole night, and the next day, from morning till evening, but they could not find a path out of the woods. They were very hungry, too, for they had nothing to eat but a few berries they found growing on the bushes here and there. At last they were so tired that their legs refused to carry them any longer, so they lay down under a tree and fell asleep.

On the third morning after they had left their father's house, they set about their wandering again, but only got deeper and deeper into the woods. Now they felt that if help did not come soon, they would perish. At midday they saw a beautiful little snow-white bird sitting on a branch. It sang so sweetly that they stopped and listened to it. When its song was finished it flapped its wings and flew on in front of them. They followed it and soon came to a little house, where the bird perched on the roof.

And when they came quite near they saw that the cottage was made of bread and roofed with cakes, while the window was made of transparent sugar.

"Now," said Hansel, "we'll have a feast. I'll eat a bit of the roof, and you, Gretel, can eat some of the window which you will find a sweet morsel."

Hansel reached up and broke off a little bit of the roof to see what it was like, and Gretel went to the window, and began to nibble at it. Immediately a shrill voice called out from the room inside:

> *"Nibble, nibble, little mouse,*
> *Who is nibbling at my house?"*

The children answered:

> *"Tis Heaven's own child,*
> *The tempest wild,"*

and went on eating without worry. Hansel, who found the roof delicious, tore down a big part of it, while Gretel pushed out an entire round windowpane and sat down to enjoy it.

Suddenly the door opened, and an ancient woman leaning on a staff hobbled out. Hansel and Gretel were so terrified that they let what they had in their hands fall. But the old woman shook her head and said:

"Oh, ho! you dear children. Who led you here? Just come in and stay with me; no ill shall befall you."

She took them both by the hand and led them into the house, and laid a most sumptuous dinner before them—milk and sugared pancakes, with apples and nuts. After they had finished, two beautiful little white beds were prepared for them. When Hansel and Gretel lay down in them they felt as if they had gone to heaven.

The woman had appeared to be most friendly, but she was really an old witch who had waylaid the children, and had only built the little bread house in order to lure them in. When anyone fell under her spell she killed, cooked, and ate them, holding a regular feast-day for the occasion. Now witches have red eyes and cannot see far, but, like beasts, they have a keen sense of smell, and know when human beings pass by. When Hansel and Gretel fell into her hands, she laughed maliciously and said:

"I've got them now; they shan't escape me."

Early in the morning, before the children were awake, the witch arose. And when she saw them both sleeping so peacefully, with their round rosy cheeks, she muttered to herself:

"That'll be a dainty bite."

Then she seized Hansel with her bony hands and carried him into a little stable, and barred the door on him. He screamed as loudly as he could, but it did him no good. Then she went to Gretel, shook her till she awoke, and cried:

"Get up, you lazy-bones, fetch water and cook something for your brother. When he's fat I'll eat him up."

Gretel began to cry bitterly, but it was of no use; she had to do what the wicked witch told her.

So the best food was cooked for poor Hansel, but Gretel got nothing but crab-shells. Every morning the old woman hobbled out to the stable and cried:

"Hansel, stick out your finger, that I may feel if you are getting fat."

But Hansel always stretched out a bone, and the old woman, whose eyes were bad, couldn't see it, and thinking it was Hansel's finger, wondered why he fattened so slowly. When four weeks passed and Hansel still remained thin, she lost patience and decided to wait no longer.

"Gretel," she called to the girl, "be quick and get some water. Hansel may be fat or thin, but I'm going to kill him tomorrow and cook him."

Oh! How the poor little sister sobbed as she carried the water, and how the tears rolled down her cheeks!

"Kind heaven help us now!" she cried. "If only the wild beasts in the woods had eaten us, then at least we should have died together."

"Just hold your peace," said the old hag. "It won't help you."

Early in the morning, Gretel had to go out and hang up the kettle full of water and light the fire.

"First we'll bake," said the witch. "I've already heated the oven and kneaded the dough."

She pushed Gretel out to the oven, from which fiery flames already leapt.

"Creep in," said the witch, "and see if it's properly heated, so that we can shove in the bread."

For when she had gotten Gretel in, the old woman meant to close the oven and let the girl bake, so that she might eat her up too. But Gretel perceived her intention, and spoke:

"I don't know how I'm to do it; how do I get in?"

"You silly goose!" said the hag, "the opening is big enough. See, I could get in myself." And she crawled toward it, and poked her head into the oven.

Then Gretel gave her a shove that sent her right in, shut the iron door, and drew the bolt. Gracious! How she yelled! It was quite horrible. But Gretel fled, and the wretched old woman was left to perish miserably.

Then Gretel ran straight to Hansel, opened the little stabledoor, and cried:

"Hansel, we are free; the old witch is dead."

Then Hansel sprang like a bird out of a cage when the door is opened. How they rejoiced, and hugged each other, and jumped for joy, and kissed one another! And as they no longer had any cause for fear, they went to the old hag's house, and there they found, in every corner of the room, boxes of pearls and precious stones.

"These are even better than pebbles," Hansel said, and filled his pockets full of them; and Gretel said:

"I too will bring some of them home." And she filled her apron full.

"Now," said Hansel, "let's go and get well away from the witch's woods."

After they had wandered about for several hours, they came to a big river.

"We can't get across it," said Hansel. "I see no bridge of any kind."

"Yes, and there's no ferry-boat either," answered Gretel. "But look, there swims a white duck; perhaps she'll help us over." So she called out:

> *"Here are two children,*
> *Mournful very,*
> *Seeing neither*
> *Bridge nor ferry;*
> *Take us upon*
> *Your white back,*
> *And row us over,*
> *Quack, quack!"*

The duck swam toward them, and Hansel got on her back and asked his little sister to sit beside him.

"No," answered Gretel, "we would be too heavy a load for the duck; she will have to carry us across separately."

The good bird did this, and when they were both safely on the other side, and had gone on for a while, the woods became more and more familiar to them, and after a while they saw their father's house in the distance.

Then they began to run, and bounding into the room, they hugged their father. The man had not passed a happy hour since he left them in the woods, but the woman had died. Gretel shook out her apron, and the pearls and precious stones rolled about the room, and Hansel also emptied his pockets one handful after another. Thus all their troubles were ended, and they all lived happily ever after.

My story is done. See! There runs a little mouse. Anyone who catches it may make himself a large fur cap out of it.

The Three Languages

Grimm

ILLUSTRATED BY Ivan Chermayeff

THERE LIVED in Switzerland an old count who had an only son. But the son was very stupid and could learn nothing, so his father said to him:

"Listen to me, my son. I can get nothing into your head, try as I may. You must go away from here. I will send you to a distinguished professor for one year."

At the end of the year, the son came home again, and his father asked:

"Now, my son, what have you learned?"

"Father, I have learned the language of dogs."

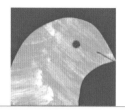

"Mercy on us!" cried his father, "is that all you have learned? I will send you away again to another professor in a different town."

The youth was taken there and remained with this professor for one more year. When he came back, his father asked him again:

"Now, my son, what have you learned?"

He answered:

"I have learned the language of birds."

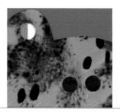

Then the father flew into a rage and said:

"Oh, you hopeless creature, have you been spending all this precious time and learned nothing? Aren't you ashamed to come into my presence? I will send you to a third professor, but if you learn nothing this time, I will not be your father any longer."

The son stayed with the third professor for another year, and when he came home again, his father asked:

"Now, my son, what have you learned?"

He answered:

"My dear father, this year I have learned the language of frogs."

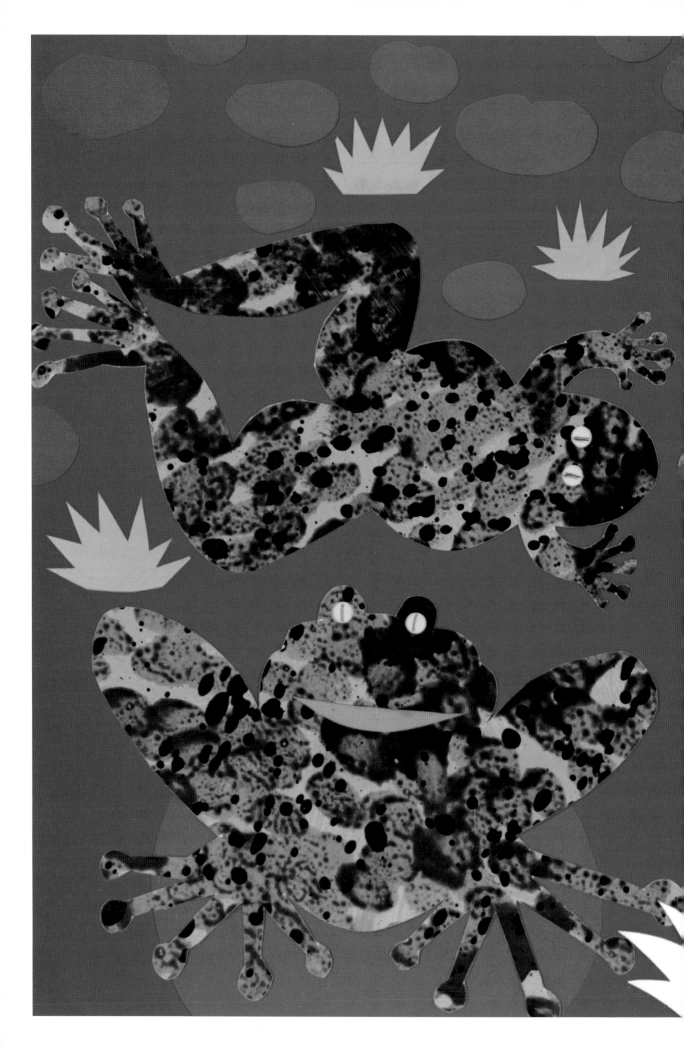

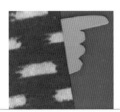

Upon hearing this, his father was filled with anger and said to his servants:

"This creature is my son no longer. I turn him out of the house and command you to lead him into the forest and take his life."

The servants took the son to the forest, but when the time came to kill him, they took pity on him and let him go. Then they cut out the eyes and tongue of a fawn, in order that they might take back proof to the old count.

The youth wandered about and at length came to a castle, where he begged for a night's lodging.

"Very well," said the lord of the castle. "If you want to spend the night down there in the old tower, you may; but I warn you that it will be at the risk of your life, for it is full of savage dogs. They bark and howl without ceasing, and at certain hours they must have a man thrown to them. Then they devour him."

The whole neighborhood was distressed by this menace, yet no one could do anything to remedy it. But the youth was not a bit afraid and said to them:

"Just let me go down to these barking dogs with something for them to eat. Then they won't do me any harm."

So they gave him some food for the savage dogs and took him down to the tower.

The dogs did not bark at the youth when he entered but ran round him, wagging their tails in a most friendly manner. They ate the food he gave them and did not so much as touch a hair of his head.

The next morning, to the surprise of everyone, the youth made his appearance again and said to the lord of the castle:

"The dogs have revealed to me in their own language why they live there and bring misery to the country. They are enchanted and obliged to guard a great treasure which is hidden under the tower.

And they will not rest until it has been dug up. I have also learned from the dogs how this task is to be done."

Everyone who heard this was delighted, and the lord of the castle said he would adopt him as a son if he accomplished the task successfully. He went down to the tower again and set to work. He accomplished his task and brought out a chest full of gold. The howling of the savage dogs was from that time forward heard no more. The beasts entirely disappeared, and the country was delivered from the terrible affliction.

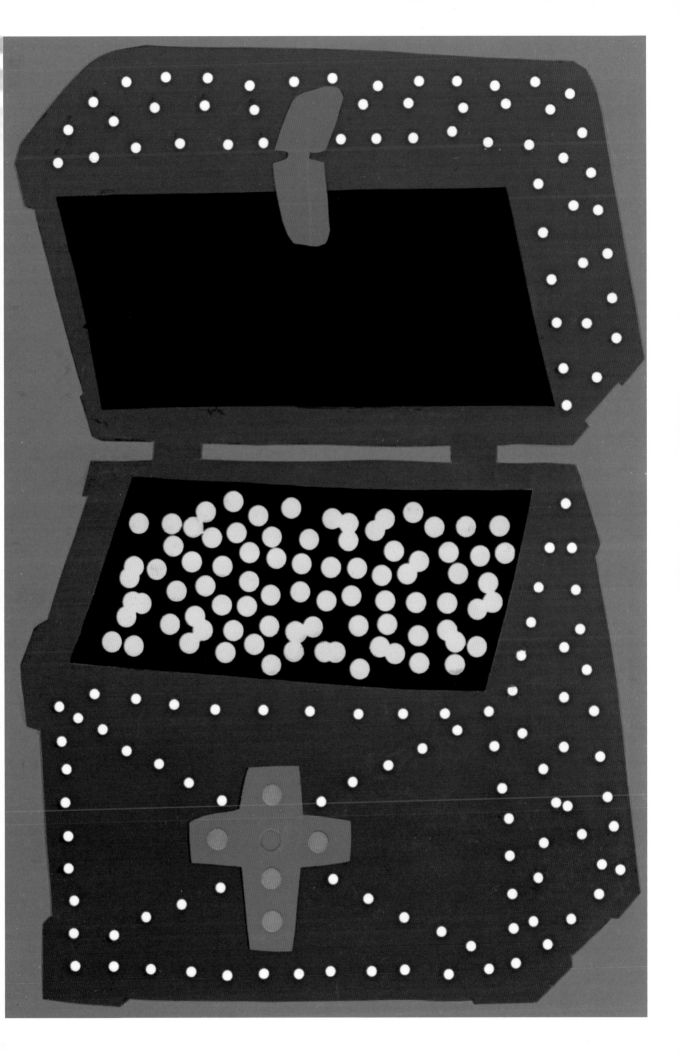

After a time, the young count took it into his head to go to Rome. On the way he passed a swamp, in which a number of frogs were croaking. He listened, and when he heard what they were saying, he became quite pensive and sad.

At last he reached Rome, at a moment when the Pope had just died, and there was great doubt among the cardinals about whom they ought to name as his successor. They agreed at last that the man to whom some divine miracle should occur ought to be chosen as Pope. Just as they had come to this decision, the young count entered the church, and suddenly two snow-white doves flew down and alighted on his shoulders.

The clergy recognized in this the sign from Heaven and asked him whether he would be Pope.

He was undecided and knew not whether he was worthy of the post; but the doves told him that he might accept, and at last he said, "Yes."

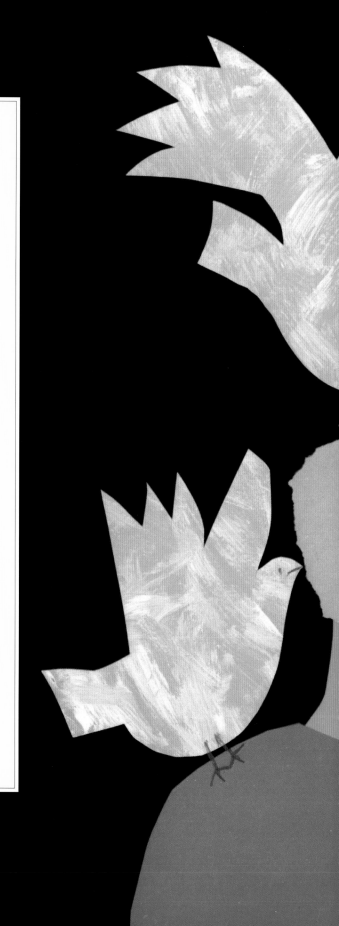

Immediately he was anointed and consecrated. The disturbing news he had heard from the frogs had indeed come to pass. He became the Pope.

When it came time for him to chant mass, he did not know one word of it. But the two doves sat upon his shoulders and whispered it to him.

THE FISHERMAN & HIS WIFE

GRIMM

ILLUSTRATED BY JOHN HOWE

ONCE UPON A TIME

THERE WAS a fisherman and his wife who lived together in a little hut close to the sea, and the fisherman used to go down every day to fish; and he would fish and fish. So he used to sit with his rod and gaze into the shining water; and he would gaze and gaze.

One day, the line was pulled deep under the water, and when he hauled it up he hauled a large flounder with it. The flounder said to him, "Listen, fisherman. I beg you to let me go; I am not a real flounder, I am an enchanted prince. What good will it do you to kill me? I shall not taste good. Put me back into the water and let me swim away."

"Well," said the man, "you need not make so much noise about it; I am sure I had better let a flounder that can talk swim away." With these words, he put him back into the shining water, and the flounder swam to the bottom, leaving a long, thin streak of blood behind. Then the

fisherman got up and went home to his wife in the hut.

"Husband," said his wife, "have you caught nothing today?"

"No," said the man. "I caught a flounder who said he was an enchanted prince, so I let him swim away."

"Did you wish nothing from him?" said his wife.

"No," said the man, "what should I have wished from him?"

"Well!" said the woman, "it's dreadful to have to live all one's life in a hut that is so small and dirty; you ought to have wished for a cottage. Go now and call him; say to him that we want a cottage, and he will certainly give it you."

"Alas!" said the man, "why should I go down there again?"

"Why," said his wife, "you caught him, and let him go, so he is sure to give you what you ask. Go quickly."

The man did not like going at all, but as his wife was not to be persuaded otherwise, he went down to the sea.

When he came to the sea it was quite green and yellow, and was no longer shining. So he stood on the shore and said:

> *"Once a prince,*
> *But changed you be*
> *Into a flounder in the sea.*
> *Come! for my wife, Ilsebel,*
> *Wishes what I dare not tell."*

Then the flounder came swimming up and said, "Well, what does she want?"

"Alas!" said the man, "my wife says I ought to have kept you and wished something from you. She does not want to live any longer in a hut; she would like a cottage."

"Go home, then," said the flounder, "she has it."

So the man went home, and in place of the hut was a beautiful cottage, and his wife was sitting in front of the door on a bench. She took him by the hand and said to him, "Come inside, and see if this is not much better."

They went in, and inside the cottage was a tiny hall, a beautiful sitting room, a bedroom, and a kitchen and a dining room all furnished with the best of everything and fitted with every kind of tin and copper utensil. Outside was a little yard with chickens and ducks, and also a little garden with vegetables and fruit trees.

"See," said the wife, "isn't this nice?"

"Yes," answered her husband, "here we shall remain and live very happily."

"We will think about that," she said.

With these words they had their supper and went to bed.

All went well for a fortnight; then the wife said:

"Listen, husband, the cottage is much too small, and so is the yard and the garden; the flounder might just as well have given us a larger house. I would like to live in a great stone castle. Go down to the flounder, and tell him to give us a castle."

"Oh, wife!" said the fisherman, "the cottage is quite good enough; why would we choose to live in a castle?"

"Why?" said the wife. "You go ask; the flounder can quite well do that."

"No, wife," said the man, "the flounder gave us this cottage. I do not want to go to him again; he might be offended."

"Go," said his wife. "He can certainly give it to us, and ought to do so willingly. Go at once."

The fisherman's heart was very heavy, and he did not like going. He said to himself, "It is not right." Still, he went.

When he came to the sea, the water was all violet and dark blue, and dull and thick, and no longer green and yellow, but it was still smooth.

So he stood there and said:

"Once a prince,
But changed you be
Into a flounder in the sea.
Come! for my wife, Ilsebel,
Wishes what I dare not tell."

"What does she want now?" said the flounder.

"Ah!" said the fisherman, half ashamed, "she wants to live in a great stone castle."

"Go home, then; she is standing before the door," said the flounder.

The fisherman went home and thought he would find no castle. When he came near, however, there stood a great stone palace, and his wife was standing on the steps, about to enter. She took him by the hand and said, "Come inside."

Then he went with her, and inside the castle was a large hall with a marble floor, and there were dozens of servants who threw open the great doors, and the walls were covered with beautiful tapestries, and in the apartments were gilded chairs and tables, and crystal chandeliers hung from the ceiling, and all the rooms were beautifully carpeted. The best of food and drink was set before them when they wished to dine. And outside the house was a large courtyard with horse and cow stables and a carriage house—all fine

buildings; and a splendid garden with the most beautiful flowers and fruit, and in a park several miles long were deer and hares, and everything one could wish for.

"Now," said the wife, "isn't this beautiful?"

"Yes, indeed," said the fisherman. "Now we will live in this beautiful castle and be very happy."

"We will consider the matter," said his wife, and they went to bed.

The next morning the wife woke up first at daybreak, and looked from the bed at the beautiful country stretched before her. Her husband was still sleeping, so she dug her elbow into his side and said: "Husband, get up and look out the window. Could we not become king of all this land? Go down to the flounder and tell him we want to be king."

"Oh, wife!" replied her husband, "why should we be king? *I* don't want to be king."

"Well," said his wife, "if you don't want to be king, *I* will be king. Go down to the flounder; I will be king."

"Alas! wife," said the fisherman, "why do you want to be king? I can't ask him that."

"And why not?" said his wife. "Go down at once. I must be king."

So the fisherman went, though much vexed that his wife wanted to be king. "It is not right! It is not right," he thought. He did not wish to go, yet he went.

When he came to the sea, the water was a dark grey color, and it was heaving against the shore. So he stood and said:

> *"Once a prince,*
> *But changed you be*
> *Into a flounder in the sea.*
> *Come! for my wife, Ilsebel,*
> *Wishes what I dare not tell."*

"What does she want now?" asked the flounder. "Alas!" said the fisherman, "she wants to be king."

"Go home, then; she is that already," said the flounder.

The fisherman went home, and when he came near the palace he saw that it had become much larger, and that it had great towers and splendid ornamental carving on it. A sentinel was standing before the gate, and there were numbers of soldiers with kettledrums and trumpets. When he went into the palace, he found that everything was of pure marble and gold, and the curtains of damask had tassels of gold.

Then the doors of the hall flew open, and there stood the whole court around his wife, who was sitting on a high throne of gold and diamonds. She wore a great golden crown and had a sceptre of gold and precious stones in her hand, and by her on either side stood six pages in a row, each one a head taller than the next. Then he went before her and said:

"Ah, wife! are you king now?"

"Yes," said his wife, "now I am king."

He stood looking at her, and when he had looked for some time, he said:

"Let that be enough, wife, now that you are king! Now we have nothing more to wish for."

"Nay, husband," said his wife restlessly, "my wishing powers are boundless; I cannot restrain them any longer. Go down to the flounder; king I am, now I must be emperor."

"Alas! wife," said the fisherman, "why do you want to be emperor?"

"Husband," she said, "go to the flounder; I *will* be emperor."

"Ah, wife," he said, "he cannot make you emperor; I don't want to ask him that. There is only one emperor in the kingdom. Indeed, he cannot make you emperor."

"What!" said his wife. "I am king, and you are my husband. You will go at once. Go! If he can make me a king he can make me an emperor, and emperor I must and will be. Go!"

So the fisherman had to go. But as he went, he felt quite frightened and thought to himself, "This can't be right; to be emperor is too ambitious; the flounder will certainly deny my request."

Thinking this he came to the shore. The sea was quite black and thick, and it was breaking high on the beach; the foam was flying about, and the wind was blowing; everything looked bleak. The fisherman was chilled with fear. He stood and said:

> *"Once a prince,*
> *But changed you be*
> *Into a flounder in the sea.*
> *Come! for my wife, Ilsebel,*
> *Wishes what I dare not tell."*

"What does she want now?" asked the flounder.

"Alas! flounder," he said, "my wife wants to be emperor."

"Go home," said the flounder, "she is that already."

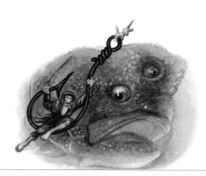

Then the fisherman went home, and when he arrived he saw the whole castle was made of polished marble, ornamented with alabaster statues and gold. Before the gate, soldiers were marching, blowing trumpets and beating drums. Inside the palace were barons, counts, and dukes acting as servants; they opened the door, which was made of beaten gold. And when he entered, he saw his wife upon a throne that was made of a single block of gold, and which was a full nine feet high. She had on a great golden crown which was likewise three yards high and set with brilliant and sparkling gems. In one hand she held a sceptre, and in the other the imperial globe. On either side of her stood two rows of armed soldiers, each smaller than the other, from a seven-foot giant to the tiniest dwarf no taller than my little finger. Many princes and dukes were standing before her. The fisherman went up to her quietly and said:

"Wife, are you emperor now?"

"Yes," she said, "I am emperor."

He stood looking at her magnificence, and when he had watched her for some time, said:

"Oh, wife, let that be enough, now that you are emperor."

"Husband," she said, "why are you standing there? I am emperor now, and I want to be pope, too; go down to the flounder."

"Alas! wife," said the fisherman, "what more do you want? You cannot be pope; there is only one pope in Christendom, and the flounder cannot make you that."

"Husband," she said, "I will be pope. Go down quickly; I must be pope today."

"No, wife," said the fisherman, "I cannot ask him that. It is not right; it is too much. The flounder cannot make you pope."

"Husband, what nonsense!" she said. "If he can make me emperor, he can make me pope, too. Go down this instant; I am emperor and you are my husband. Be off at once!"

So he was frightened and went out; but he felt quite faint and trembled and shook, and his legs began to give way under him. The wind was blowing fiercely across the land, and the clouds flying across the sky looked as gloomy as if it were night; the leaves were being blown from the trees; the water was foaming and seething and dashing upon the shore, and in the distance the fisherman saw the ships in great distress, dancing and tossing on the waves. Still the sky was very blue in the middle, although at the sides it was an angry red as in a great storm. So he stood shuddering in anxiety, and said:

> *"Once a prince,*
> *But changed you be*
> *Into a flounder in the sea.*
> *Come! for my wife, Ilsebel*
> *Wishes what I dare not tell."*

"Well, what does she want now?" asked the flounder.

"Alas!" said the fisherman, "she wants to be pope."

"Go home, then; she is that already," said the flounder.

Then he went home, and when he arrived there he saw, as it were, a large church surrounded by palaces. He pushed his way through the people. The interior was lit up with thousands and thousands of candles, and his wife was dressed in cloth of gold and was sitting on a much higher throne, and she wore three great golden crowns. Around her were a number of Church dignitaries, and on either side were standing two rows of candles, the largest of them as tall as a steeple, and the smallest as tiny as a Christmas tree candle. All the emperors and kings were on their knees before her, and were kissing her foot.

"Wife," said the fisherman, "are you pope now?"

"Yes," said she, "I am pope."

So he stood staring at her, and it was as if he were looking at the bright sun. When he had watched her for some time he said:

"Ah, wife, let it be enough now that you are pope."

But she sat as straight as a tree and did not move or bend the least bit. He said again:

"Wife, be content that you are pope. You cannot become anything more."

"We will think about that," she said.

With these words they went to bed. But the woman was not content. Her greed would not allow her to sleep, and she kept on thinking and thinking what she could still become. The fisherman slept well and soundly, for he had done a great deal that day, but his wife could not sleep at all. She turned from one side to the other the whole night long, and thought till she could think no longer, what more she could become. Then the sun began to rise, and when she saw the red dawn she went to the end of the bed and looked at it, and as she was watching the sun rise, she thought, "Ha! could I not make the sun and moon rise?"

"Husband," she said, poking him in the ribs with her elbow, "wake up. Go down to the flounder; I must be a god."

The fisherman was still half asleep, yet was so frightened that he fell out of bed. He thought he had not heard correctly, and opened his eyes wide and said:

"What did you say, wife?"

"Husband," she said, "if I cannot make the sun and moon rise when I appear, I cannot rest. I shall never have a peaceful moment till I can make the sun and moon rise."

He looked at her in horror, and a shudder ran over him.

"Go down at once," she said. "I must be a god."

"Alas! wife," said the fisherman, falling on his knees before her, "the flounder cannot do that. Emperor and pope he has made you. I implore you, be content and remain pope."

Then she flew into a rage, her hair flinging wildly about her face, and she pushed him with her foot and screamed:

"I am not contented, and I shall not be contented! You will go!"

So he quickly put on his clothes, and dashed madly from the palace.

But the storm was raging so
fiercely that he could scarcely stand.
Houses and trees were being blown
down, the mountains were being
shaken, and pieces of rock were
rolling into the sea. The sky was as
black as ink, it was thundering and
lightning, and the sea was tossing in
great waves as high as church towers
and mountains, and each had a white
crest of foam.

So he shouted, not able to hear
his own voice:

> *"Once a prince,*
> *But changed you be*
> *Into a flounder in the sea*
> *Come! for my wife, Ilsebel,*
> *Wishes what I dare not tell."*

"Well, what does she want
now?" asked the flounder.

"Alas!" the fisherman said, "she
wants to be a god."

"Go home, then; she is sitting
again in the hut."

And there they are sitting to this
day.

THE QUEEN BEE

GRIMM

ILLUSTRATED BY PHILIPPE DUMAS

Two PRINCES started off in search of adventure and, falling into a wild, free way of life, did not come home.

A third brother, the youngest, set out to look for the other two. But when at last he found them, they mocked him for thinking he could make his way in the world with his simplicity, while they, who were so much more clever, could not even make it.

All three went on together till they came to an anthill. The two elder princes wanted to disturb it, to see how the little ants crept away, carrying their eggs.

But the third prince said: "Leave the little creatures alone. I will not allow you to disturb them."

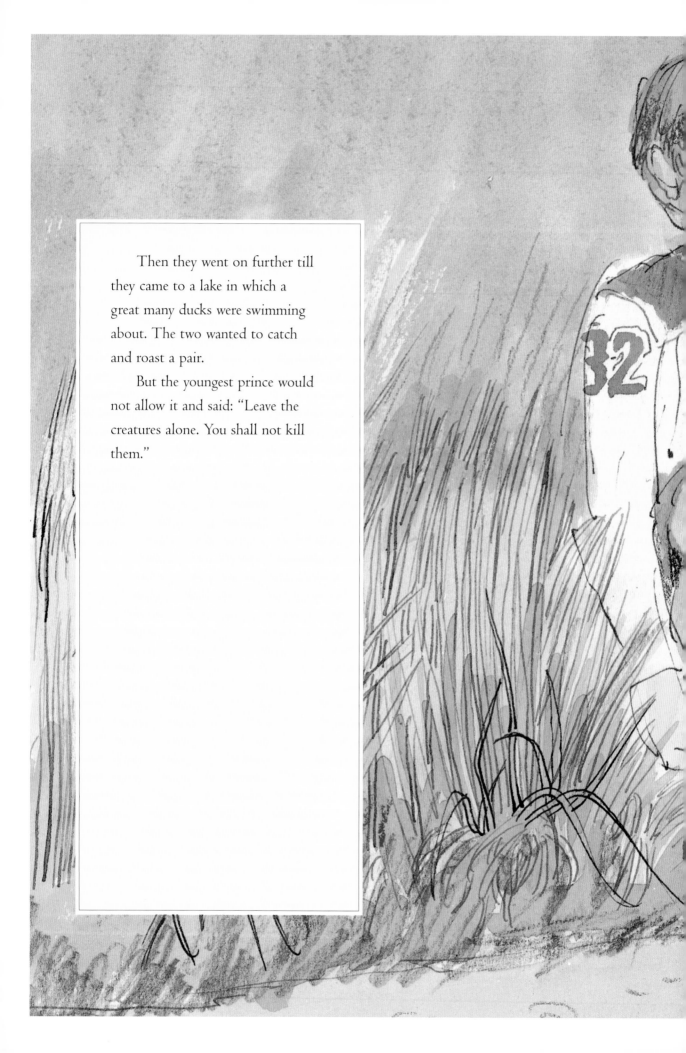

Then they went on further till they came to a lake in which a great many ducks were swimming about. The two wanted to catch and roast a pair.

But the youngest prince would not allow it and said: "Leave the creatures alone. You shall not kill them."

At last they came to a bees' nest containing such a vast quantity of honey that it flowed round the trunk of the tree.

The two princes wanted to set fire to the tree and suffocate the bees, so as to remove the honey.

But the youngest prince stopped them again and said: "Leave the creatures alone. I will not let you burn them."

At last the three brothers came
to a castle, where the stables were
full of stone horses but not a soul
was to be seen. They went through
all the rooms till they came to a door
quite at the far end, fastened with
three bolts. In the middle of the
door was a lattice, through which
one could see into the room.

There they saw a little grey man sitting at a table. They called to him once—and then twice—but he did not hear them. Finally, when they had called him the third time, he stood up, opened the door, and came out. He said not a word but led them to a richly spread table, and when they had eaten and drunk, he took them each to a bedroom.

The next morning, the little grey man came to the eldest prince, beckoned, and led him to a stone tablet whereon were inscribed three tasks by means of which the castle should be freed from enchantment.

This was the first task: In the woods, under the moss, lay the princesses' pearls, a thousand in number. These had to all be found, and if at sunset a single one were missing, the seeker would be turned to stone.

The eldest went away and searched all day, but when evening came, he had found only the first hundred, and it happened as the inscription foretold. He was turned to stone.

The next day the second brother undertook the quest. But he fared no better than the first, for he found only two hundred pearls, and he too was turned to stone.

At last the third brother's turn came. He searched in the moss, but the pearls were hard to find, and he worked slowly.

Then he sat down on a rock and cried. But as he was sitting there, the Ant King, whose life he had saved, came up with five thousand ants, and it was not long before the little creatures had found all the pearls and laid them in a heap.

Now the second task was to get
the key to the princesses' room
out of the lake.

When the youngest prince came
to the lake, the ducks he had once
saved swam up, dived, and brought
up the key from the depths.

But the third task was the hardest. The prince had to find out which was the youngest and most charming of the princesses while they were asleep.

They were exactly alike and could not be distinguished in any way, except that before going to sleep, each had eaten a different kind of sweet. The eldest had a piece of sugar, the second a little syrup, and the youngest a spoonful of honey.

Then the Queen of the Bees, whom the youngest prince had saved from burning, came and tasted the lips of all three. She settled on the mouth of the one who had eaten the honey, and so the prince recognized the right one.

Then the charm was broken and everything in the castle was set free, and those who had been turned to stone took human form again.

And the youngest prince married the youngest and sweetest princess and became King after her father's death, while his two brothers married the other sisters.

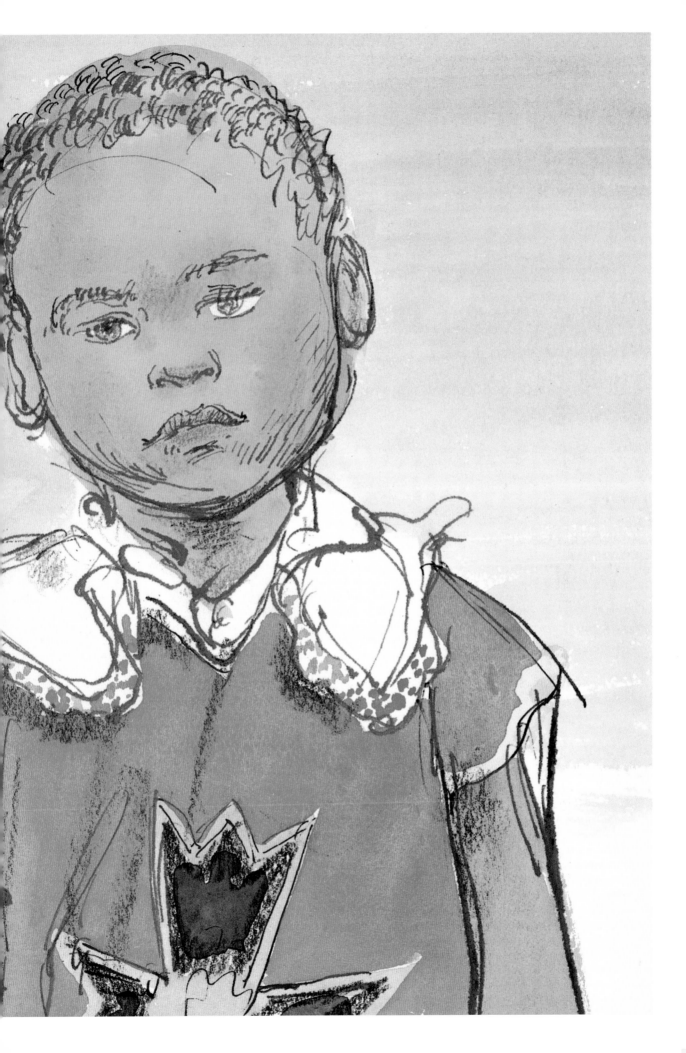

BUSHY BRIDE

NORWEGIAN FAIRY TALE
ILLUSTRATED BY SEYMOUR CHWAST

THERE WAS a widower who had a son and a daughter by his first wife. They were both good children and loved each other with all their hearts. After some time had gone by, the man married again, and he chose a widow with one daughter who was ugly and wicked, and her mother was ugly and wicked too. From the very day that the new wife came into the house, there was no peace for the man's children, and not a corner to be found where they could get any rest. So the boy thought that the best thing he could do was to go out into the world and earn his own bread.

When he had roamed about for some time, he came to the King's palace, where he obtained a place under the coachman. So brisk and active was the boy at his work that the horses he looked after were fat and sleek and shiny.

But his sister, who was still at home, fared worse and worse. Both her stepmother and her stepsister were always finding fault with her, whatever she did and wherever she went. And they scolded her and abused her so that she never had an hour's peace. They made her do all the hard work of the house, and harsh words fell on her early and late, but little enough food accompanied them.

One day they sent her to the brook to fetch some water, and an ugly and horrible head rose up out of the water and said, "Wash me, girl!"

"Yes, I will wash you with pleasure," said the girl, and she began to wash and scrub the ugly face, but she couldn't help thinking that it was a very unpleasant piece of work. When she had done it, and done it well, another head rose up out of the water, and this one was uglier still.

"Brush me, girl!" said the head.

"Yes, I will brush you with pleasure," said the girl, and she set to work on the tangled hair. As may be easily imagined, this too was by no means very pleasant work.

When she had at last gotten it done, another and a much more ugly and horrible-looking head rose up out of the water.

"Kiss me, girl!" said the head.

"Yes, I will kiss you," said the girl, and she did it, but she thought it was the worst bit of work that she had ever had to do in her life.

So the heads all began to talk to each other and to ask what they should do for this girl who was so full of kindliness.

"She shall be the prettiest girl that ever was and fair and bright as the day," said the first head.

"Gold shall drop from her hair whenever she brushes it," said the second.

"Gold shall drop from her mouth whenever she speaks," said the third head.

So when the man's daughter went home, looking as beautiful and bright as day, the stepmother and her daughter grew much more ill-tempered, and it was worse still when she began to talk and they saw that golden coins dropped from her mouth. The stepmother fell into such a towering rage that she drove the man's daughter into the pigsty. She might stay there with her fine show of gold, the stepmother said, but she should not be permitted to set foot in the house.

It was not long before the mother wanted her own daughter to go to the stream to fetch some water.

When the girl got there with her pails, the first head rose up out of the water close to the bank.

"Wash me, girl!" it said.

"Wash yourself!" answered the woman's daughter.

Then the second head came up out of the water.

"Brush me, girl!" said the head.

"Brush yourself!" said the girl.

So down it went to the bottom, and the third head came up.

"Kiss me, girl!" said the head.

"As if I would kiss your ugly mouth!" said the girl.

So again the heads talked together about what they should do for this girl who was so ill-tempered and full of her own importance, and they agreed that she should have a nose that was four feet long, and a jaw that was three feet, and a fir bush in the middle of her forehead, and every time she spoke, ashes should fall from her mouth.

When she came back to the cottage door with her pails, she called to her mother, who was inside, "Open the door!"

"Open the door yourself, my own dear child!" said the mother.

"I can't get near because of my nose," said the daughter.

When the mother came and saw her, you may imagine what a state of mind she was in, and how she screamed and lamented, but neither the nose nor the jaw grew any the less for it.

Now the brother, who was in service in the King's palace, had taken a portrait of his sister, and he had carried the picture with him. Every morning and evening, he knelt down before it and prayed for his sister, so dearly did he love her.

The other stableboys had heard him doing this, so they peeped through the keyhole into his room and saw that he was kneeling there before a picture. They told everyone that every morning and evening the youth knelt down and prayed to an idol. And at last they went to the King himself and begged that he too would peep through the keyhole and see for himself what the youth did. At first the King would not believe this. But after a long time, they prevailed upon him, and he crept on tiptoe to the door, peeped through, and saw the youth on his knees with his hands clasped together before a picture on a small table.

"Open the door!" cried the King, but the youth did not hear.

"Open the door, I say!" cried the King again. "It is I! I want to come in."

So the youth sprang to the door and unlocked it, but in his haste, he forgot to hide the picture.

When the King entered and saw it, he stood still, as if he were bound by chains and could not stir from the spot, for the young woman in the picture seemed to him so beautiful.

"There is nowhere on earth so beautiful a woman as this!" said the King.

But the youth told him that she was his sister, and that he had painted her, and that if she was not prettier than the picture, she was certainly not uglier.

"Well, if she is as beautiful as that, I will have her for my queen," said the King, and he commanded the youth to go home and fetch her without a moment's delay and to lose no time in coming back.

The youth promised to make all the haste he could and set forth from the King's palace.

When the brother arrived at home to fetch his sister, her stepmother and stepsister wanted to go too. So they all set out together, and the man's daughter took with her a casket in which she kept her gold, and a dog called Little Snow. These two things were all that she had inherited from her mother. After they had traveled for some time, they had to cross the sea. The brother sat down at the helm, and the mother and the two stepsisters went to the bow of the vessel, and they sailed a long, long way.

At last they came in sight of land.

"Look at that white beach there; that is where we shall land," said the brother, pointing across the sea.

"What is my brother saying?" inquired the man's daughter.

"He says that you are to throw your casket out into the sea," answered the stepmother.

"Well, if my brother says so, I must do it," said the man's daughter, and she flung her casket into the sea.

When they had sailed for some time longer, the brother once more pointed over the sea.

"There you may see the palace to which we are bound," said he.

"What is my brother saying?" asked the man's daughter.

"Now he says that you are to throw your dog into the sea," answered the stepmother.

The man's daughter wept and was sorely troubled, for Little Snow was the dearest thing she had on earth, but at last she threw him overboard.

"If my brother says that, I must do it, but Heaven knows how unwilling I am to throw you out, Little Snow!" said she.

So they sailed onward a long way farther.

"There you may see the King coming out to meet you," said the brother, pointing to the seashore.

"What is my brother saying?" asked his sister again.

"Now he says that you are to quickly throw yourself overboard," answered the stepmother.

She wept and she wailed, but as her brother had said that, she thought she must do it. So she leaped into the sea.

When they arrived at the palace, and the King beheld the ugly bride with a nose that was four feet long, a jaw that was three feet, and a forehead that had a bush in the middle of it, he was quite terrified. But the wedding feast was all prepared and all the wedding guests were sitting in wait, so, ugly as she was, the King was forced to take her.

But the King was very angry, and none can blame him for that, so he had the brother thrown into a pit full of snakes.

On the first Thursday night after this, a beautiful maiden came into the kitchen of the palace and begged the kitchen maid, who slept there, to lend her a brush. She begged very prettily and got it, and then she brushed her hair, and gold dropped from it.

A little dog was with her, and she said to it, "Go out, Little Snow, and see if it will soon be day!"

This she said three times, and the third time that she sent out the dog to see, it was very near dawn. Then she had to depart, but as she went, she said:

"Shame on you,
Ugly Bushy Bride,
Sleeping so soft
By the young King's side,
On sand and stones,
My bed I make,
And my brother sleeps

With the cold snake,
Unpitied and unwept."

"I shall come twice more and then never again," said she.

In the morning, the kitchen maid related what she had seen and heard, and the King said that next Thursday night he himself would watch in the kitchen and see if this were true, and when it had begun to grow dark, he went out into the kitchen to see the maiden. But though he rubbed his eyes and did everything he could to keep himself awake, it was all in vain, for the Bushy Bride crooned and sang till his eyes were fast closed. When the beautiful young maiden came, he was sound asleep and snoring.

This time also, as before, she borrowed a brush and brushed her hair with it, and gold dropped down as she did it. And again she sent the dog out three times, and when day dawned, she departed. But as she was going, she said, "I shall come once more and then never again."

On the third Thursday night, the King once more insisted on keeping watch. He ordered two men to hold him; each of them was to take an arm and shake him and jerk him whenever he seemed to be falling asleep. He also ordered two men to watch his Bushy Bride. But as the night wore on, the Bushy Bride again began to croon and sing so that his eyes began to close and his head to droop on one side. Then came the lovely maiden. She got the brush and brushed her hair till gold dropped from it, and then she sent her Little Snow out to see if it would soon be day, and this she did three times. The third time it was just beginning to grow light, and then she said:

"Shame on you,
Ugly Bushy Bride,
Sleeping so soft
By the young King's side,
On sand and stones
My bed I make,
And my brother sleeps
With the cold snake,
Unpitied and unwept."

"Now I shall never come again," she said, and then she turned to go. But the two men who were holding the King by the arms seized his hands and forced a knife into his grasp, and then they made him cut the maiden's little finger just enough to make it bleed.

Thus the true bride was freed. The King then awoke, and she told him all that had taken place, and how her stepmother and stepsister had betrayed her. Then the brother was at once taken out of the snake pit—the snakes had never touched him—and the stepmother and step-sister were flung down into it instead.

The King was delighted to get rid of that hideous Bushy Bride and to get a queen who was bright and beautiful as day itself.

And then the real wedding was held, and held in such a way that it was heard of and spoken about all over seven kingdoms. The King and his bride drove to church, and Little Snow was in the carriage too. When the blessing was given, they went home again, and after that I saw no more of them.

THE SLEEPING BEAUTY

PERRAULT

ILLUSTRATED BY JOHN COLLIER

Once upon a time

THERE LIVED a king and a queen who were so sorry that they had no children; so sorry that it cannot be expressed. They went to all the waters in the world; vows, pilgrimages, all ways were tried, and all to no avail.

At last, however, the Queen had a daughter. There was a very fine baptism; and the Princess had for her godmothers all the fairies they could find in the whole kingdom (they found seven), that every one of them might give her a gift, as was the custom of fairies in those days.

After the ceremonies of the baptism were over, the whole company returned to the King's palace, where there was prepared a great feast for the fairies. There was arranged before every one of them a magnificent place setting with a cover of gold, wherein were a spoon, knife, and fork, all of pure gold and set with diamonds and rubies. But as they were all sitting down at the table, they saw come into the hall a very old fairy, whom they had not invited because it had been over fifty years since she had been out of a certain tower and she was believed to be either dead or enchanted.

The King ordered her a place setting but could not furnish her with a cover of gold as the others, because they had made only seven for the seven fairies. The old fairy fancied she was slighted and muttered some threats between her teeth. One of the young fairies who sat by her overheard how she grumbled; and, judging that she might give the little Princess some unlucky gift, the young fairy went, as soon as they rose from table, and hid herself behind the hangings, that she might speak last and repair, as much as she could, the evil that the old fairy might intend.

In the meantime, all the fairies began to give their gifts to the Princess. The youngest said that the Princess should be the most beautiful person in the world; the next, that she should have the wit of an angel; the third, that she should have a wonderful grace in everything she did; the fourth, that she should dance perfectly well; the fifth, that she should sing like a nightingale; and the sixth, that she should play all kinds of music to the utmost perfection.

The old fairy's turn came next. With a head shaking more with spite than age, she said that the Princess should have her hand pierced with a spindle and die of the wound. This terrible gift made the whole company tremble, and everyone began to weep.

At this very instant, the young fairy came out from behind the hangings and said these words aloud:

"Assure yourselves, O King and Queen, that your daughter shall not die of this disaster. It is true, I have no power to undo entirely what my elder has done. The Princess shall indeed pierce her hand with a spindle; but, instead of dying, she shall only fall into a profound sleep, which shall last a hundred years, at the expiration of which a king's son shall come and awake her."

The King, to avoid the misfortune foretold by the old fairy, immediately made a proclamation whereby all in the kingdom were forbidden, on pain of death, to spin with a distaff and spindle or to have so much as any spindle in their houses.

About fifteen or sixteen years after, the King and Queen being away one day, the young Princess happened to entertain herself by running up and down the palace. When going up from one apartment to another, she came into a little room on the top of the tower where a good old woman, alone, was spinning with her spindle. This old woman had never heard of the King's proclamation against spindles.

"What are you doing there?" asked the Princess.

"I am spinning, my pretty child," said the old woman, who did not know who the Princess was.

"Ha!" said the Princess, "this is very pretty; how do you do it? Give it to me, that I may see if I can do it."

She had no sooner taken the spindle into her hand than, whether being very hasty at it, somewhat clumsy, or that the decree of the fairy had so ordained it, it ran into her hand, and she fell down in a swoon.

The old woman, not knowing what to do, cried out for help. People came in from every quarter in great numbers; they threw water upon the Princess's face, unlaced her corset, struck her on the palms of her hands, and rubbed her temples, but nothing would bring her to herself.

And now the King, who came up at the noise, remembered the prediction of the fairies, and, judging that this must necessarily come to pass, since the fairies had said it, had the Princess carried into the finest apartment in his palace and laid upon a bed all embroidered with gold and silver.

One would have taken the Princess for a little angel, she was so very beautiful; for her swooning away had not diminished one bit of her complexion. Her cheeks were carnation, and her lips were coral; indeed her eyes were shut, but she was heard to breathe softly, which satisfied those about her that she was not dead. The King commanded that they should not disturb her, but let her sleep quietly till her hour of waking had come.

The good fairy who had saved the girl's life by condemning her to sleep a hundred years was in the kingdom of Matakin, twelve thousand leagues off, when this accident befell the Princess. But she was instantly informed of it by a little dwarf who had boots of seven leagues—that is, boots with which he could tread over seven leagues of ground in one stride. The fairy left immediately, and she arrived, about an hour after, in a fiery chariot drawn by dragons.

The King helped her out of the chariot, and she approved everything he had done. But as she had very great foresight, she thought when the Princess should awake she might not know what to do with herself, being all alone in this old palace; and this was what she did: she touched with her wand everything in the palace (except the King and the Queen)— governesses, maids of honor, chambermaids, gentlemen, officers, stewards, cooks, waiters, guards, soldiers, pages, and servants; she likewise touched the horses which were in the stables, the great dogs in the outward court, and pretty little Mopsey too, the Princess's little spaniel, which lay by her on the bed.

Immediately upon her touching them, they all fell asleep, that they might not wake before their mistress, and that they might be ready to wait upon her when she wanted them. The very spits at the fire, as full as they could hold of partridges and pheasants, did fall asleep also. All of this enchantment was done in

a moment. Fairies are not long in doing their business.

And now the King and the Queen, having kissed their dear child without waking her, went out of the palace and put forth a proclamation that nobody should dare to come near it.

This, however, was not necessary, for in a quarter of an hour's time there grew up all around such a vast number of trees, great and small, bushes and brambles, twining one within another, that neither man nor beast could pass through; so that nothing could be seen but the very top of the towers of the palace (and that, too, not unless it was a good way off). Nobody doubted that the fairy gave a very extraordinary showing of her power, so that the Princess, while she continued sleeping, might have nothing to fear from any curious people.

When a hundred years were gone and passed, the son of the king then reigning, who was of another family from that of the sleeping Princess, being gone a-hunting on that side of the country, asked what those towers were which he saw in the middle of a great thick woods. All answered according to what they had heard. Some said that it was a ruinous old castle, haunted by spirits. Others, that all the sorcerers and witches of the country kept their sabbath or night's meeting there. The common opinion was that an ogre lived there, and that he carried there all the little children he could catch, that he might eat them up at his leisure, without anybody being able to follow him, having himself only the power to pass through the woods.

The Prince did not know what to believe, when a very aged countryman said to him:

"May it please your royal highness, it is now about fifty years since I heard from my father, who heard my grandfather say, that there was then in this castle a princess, the most beautiful was ever seen; that she must sleep there a hundred years and should be waked by a king's son for whom she was reserved."

The young Prince was all on fire at these words, believing, without weighing the matter, that he could put an end to the Princess's slumber; and, pushed on by love and honor, he resolved that moment to look into it.

Barely had he advanced toward the woods when all the great trees, the bushes, and brambles gave way to let him pass through; he walked up to the castle, which he saw at the end of a large avenue, and he was surprised that none of his people could follow him, because the trees closed again as soon as he had passed through them. However, he did not cease from continuing his way; a young and amorous prince is always valiant.

He came into a spacious outward court, where everything he saw might have frozen up the most fearless person with horror. There reigned over all a most frightful silence; the image of death everywhere showed itself. There was nothing to be seen but stretched-out bodies of men and animals, all seeming to be dead. He, however, very well knew, by the ruby faces and pimpled noses of the soldiers, that they were only asleep; and their goblets, wherein still remained some drops of wine, showed plainly why they were all asleep.

He then crossed a court paved with marble, went up the stairs, and came into the guard chamber, where guards were standing in their ranks, with their muskets upon their shoulders, and snoring as loudly as they could. After that, he went through several rooms full of gentlemen and ladies, all asleep, some standing, others sitting. At last he came into a chamber all gilded with gold, where he saw upon a bed, the curtains of which were all open, the finest sight was ever beheld—a princess, who appeared to be about fifteen or sixteen years of age, and whose bright and resplendent beauty seemed nothing less than divine. He approached with trembling and admiration and fell down before her on his knees.

And now, as the enchantment was at an end, the Princess awoke and looked on the young man with eyes more tender than the first view might seem to suggest.

"Is it you, my Prince?" she said to him. "You have waited a long while."

The Prince, charmed with these words, and much more with the manner in which they were spoken, knew not how to show his joy and gratitude; he assured her that he loved her more than he did himself. Their happy talk did not make much sense, and they did weep more than talk—little eloquence, a great deal of love. He was more at a loss than she, and one need not wonder at it. She had time to think on what to say to him, for it is very probable (though history mentions nothing of it) that the good fairy, during so long a sleep, had given her very agreeable dreams. They talked four hours together, and yet they said not half what they had to say.

In the meantime, all the palace awoke; everyone set about their business, and as all of them were not in love, they were ready to die of hunger. The chief lady of honor, being as hungry as anyone, grew very impatient and told the Princess loudly that supper was served. The Prince helped the Princess to rise; she was entirely dressed, and very magnificently, but his royal highness took care not to tell her that she was dressed like his great-grandmother and had a point band peeping over a high collar. Yet she looked not a bit the less charming and beautiful for all that.

They went into the great hall of mirrors, where they dined and were served by the Princess's officers; the violins and oboes played old tunes, but very excellent, though it was now over a hundred years since they had played. After supper, without losing any time, the minister married them in the chapel of the castle, and the chief lady of honor drew the curtains. They had but very little sleep—the Princess had no need of it, and the Prince left her the next morning to return to the city, where his father was worried about him. The Prince told him that he lost his way in the forest as he was hunting, and that he had lain in the cottage of a charcoal-burner who gave him cheese and brown bread.

The King, his father, who was a good man, believed him; but his mother could not be persuaded it was true, and seeing that he went a-hunting almost every day, and that he always had some excuse ready for so doing, and that he often stayed out three or four nights at a time, she began to suspect that he was married. He lived with the Princess over two whole years and had by her two children, the eldest of which, who was a daughter, was named Morning, and the youngest, who was a son, they called Day, because he was a great deal handsomer and more beautiful than his sister.

The Queen spoke several times to her son to learn after what manner he did pass his time, demanding that he ought in duty to satisfy her curiosity.

But he never dared to trust her with his secret; he feared her, though he loved her, for she was of the race of the ogres, and the King would never have married her had it not been for her vast riches. It was even whispered about the court that she had ogreish inclinations, and that whenever she saw little children passing by, she had all the difficulty in the world to keep from falling upon them. And so the Prince would never tell her one word.

But when the King died, which happened about two years later, and he saw himself become lord and master, the Prince openly declared his marriage; and he went in great ceremony to bring his wife to the palace. They made a magnificent entry into the capital city, she riding between her two children.

Soon after, the new King went to war with the emperor Contalabutte, his neighbor. He left the government of the kingdom to the elder Queen, his mother, and left in her care his wife and children. He was obliged to continue his expedition all the summer, and as soon as he departed, the Queen mother sent her daughter-in-law to a country house among the woods, that she might more easily gratify her horrible longing.

Some few days afterwards, she said to her cook:

"I have a mind to eat little Morning for my dinner tomorrow."

"Ah! madam," cried the cook.

"I will have it so," replied the Queen (and this she spoke in the tone of an ogress who had a strong desire to eat fresh meat), "and will eat her with a sauce Robert."

The poor man, knowing very well that he must not play games with ogresses, took his great knife and went up into little Morning's chamber. She was then four years old, and she came up to him jumping and laughing, to hug him about the neck and ask him for some sugar candy. Upon which he began to weep, the great knife fell out of his hand, and he went into the back yard and killed a little lamb and dressed it with such good sauce that the old Queen assured him she had never eaten anything so good in her life. He had at the same time taken little Morning to his wife, to conceal her in the lodging he had in the courtyard.

About eight days later, the wicked Queen said to the cook, "I will dine upon little Day."

He answered not a word, being resolved to cheat her as he had done before. He went to find little Day and saw him with a stick in his hand, with which he was fencing with a great monkey, the child being then only three years of age. He took him up in his arms and carried him to his wife, that she might conceal the boy in her chamber along with his sister. Then he cooked up a young, very tender goat, which the ogress found to be wonderfully good.

This was until this time all mighty well; but one evening, the wicked old Queen said to her cook:

"I will eat the Queen with the same sauce I had with her children."

It was now that the poor cook despaired of being able to deceive her. The young Queen was twenty years of age, not reckoning the hundred years she had been asleep; and how to find in the yard a beast so firm was what puzzled him. He then resolved, that he might save his own life, to cut the young Queen's throat; and going up into her chamber, with intent to do it at once, he put himself into as great a fury as he possibly could and came into the young Queen's room with his dagger in his hand. He would not, however, surprise her, but told her, with a great deal of respect, the orders he had received from the Queen mother.

"Do it," she said, stretching out her neck. "Execute your orders, and then I shall go and see my children, my poor children, whom I so much and so tenderly loved."

She thought them dead ever since they had been taken away without her knowledge.

"No, no, madam," cried the poor cook, all in tears, "you shall not die, and you shall see your children again. But you must go home with me to my lodgings, where I have concealed them, and I shall deceive the Queen once more by giving her in your stead a young deer."

Upon this he led her to his chamber, and, leaving her to embrace her children, he went and dressed a young deer, which the Queen mother had for her supper, devouring it with the same appetite as if it had been the young Queen. She was exceedingly delighted with her cruelty, and she had invented a story to tell the King, at his return, how mad wolves had eaten up the Queen his wife and her two children.

One evening, as the old Queen was, according to her custom, rambling round about the courts and yards of the palace to see if she could smell any fresh meat, she heard, in a ground room, little Day crying, for his mama was going to whip him because he had been naughty; and she heard, at the same time, little Morning begging pardon for her brother.

The ogress knew the voice of the young Queen and her children, and being quite vexed that she had been thus deceived, she commanded with a most horrible voice that made everyone tremble, that next morning, by break of day, they should bring into the middle of the great court a large tub filled with toads, vipers, snakes, and all sorts of serpents. And that the Queen and her children, the cook, and his wife and maid all be brought there with their hands tied behind them and thrown into the tub.

They were brought out accordingly, and the executioners were just going to throw them into the tub, when the King (who was not expected so soon) entered the court on horseback and asked, with the utmost astonishment, what was the meaning of that horrible spectacle.

No one dared to tell him, but the ogress, enraged to see what had happened, threw herself head first into the tub and was instantly devoured by the ugly creatures. The King could not help being sorry, for she was his mother, but he soon comforted himself with his beautiful wife and his pretty children.

THE ENCHANTED PIG

RUMANIAN FAIRY TALE
ILLUSTRATED BY JACQUES TARDI

THERE WAS a king who had three daughters. Now it happened that he had to go out to battle, so he called his daughters and said to them:

"My dear children, I am obliged to go to war. The enemy is approaching us with a large army. It is a great grief to me to leave you all. During my absence, take care of yourselves and be good girls. Look after everything in the house. You may walk in the garden, and you may go into all the rooms in the palace except the room at the back in the right-hand corner. You must not enter it, for harm would befall you."

"Don't worry, father," they replied. "We have never been disobedient to you. Go in peace, and may Heaven give you a glorious victory!"

When everything was ready for his departure, the King gave them the keys to all the rooms and reminded them once more of what he had said. His daughters kissed his hands with tears in their eyes and wished him well.

Now when the girls found themselves alone, they felt so sad that they did not know what to do. To pass the time, they decided to work for part of the day, to read for part of the day, and to enjoy themselves in the garden for part of the day. But every day they grew more and more curious.

"Sisters," said the eldest princess, "all day long we sew, spin, and read. We have been several days quite alone. We have been in all the rooms of our father's palace and have admired the beautiful furniture. Why should we not go into the room that our father forbade us to enter?"

"Sister," said the youngest, "how can you tempt us to break our father's command? When he told us not to go into that room, he must have known what he was saying."

"Surely the sky won't fall on our heads if we do go in," said the second princess. "How will our father ever find out that we have gone in?"

While they were speaking like this, encouraging each other, they reached the room. The eldest fitted the key into the lock, and snap! the door stood open.

The three girls entered, and what do you think they saw?

The room was quite empty, but in the middle stood a large table, and on it lay a big open book.

Now the princesses were curious to know what was written in the book, especially the eldest, and this is what she read:

"The eldest daughter of this King will marry a prince from the East."

Then the second girl stepped forward, and turning over the page, she read:

"The second daughter of this King will marry a prince from the West."

But the youngest princess did not want to open the book. Her sisters dragged her up to the table, and in fear and trembling, she turned the page and read:

"The youngest daughter of this King will be married to a pig from the North."

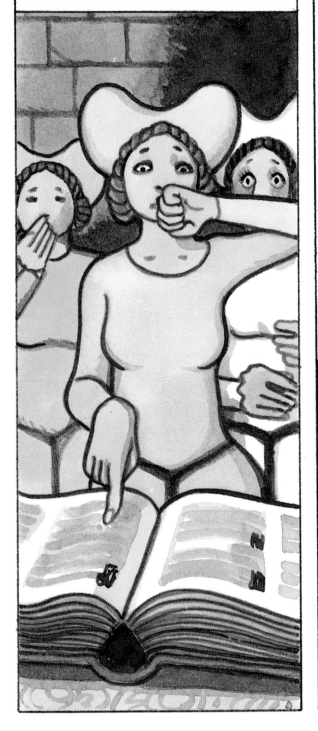

Now if a thunderbolt had fallen upon her, it would not have frightened her more. She almost died of misery. Her sisters tried to comfort her, saying:

"How can you believe such nonsense? When did it ever happen that a king's daughter married a pig?"

The youngest princess would gladly have let herself be convinced by her sisters' words. But her thoughts kept turning to the book.

Besides, the thought weighed on her heart that she was guilty of disobeying her father. She began to get quite ill, and in a few days she was so changed that it was difficult to recognize her. Formerly she had been rosy and merry; now she was pale and nothing gave her any joy. She gave up playing with her sisters in the garden and ceased to gather flowers.

In the meantime, the King won a great victory, and he hurried home to his daughters, to whom his thoughts had constantly turned. Everyone went out to meet him, and there was great rejoicing. The King's first act on reaching home was to thank Heaven for his victory in battle. He then entered his palace, and his joy was great when he saw that the princesses were all well, for the youngest did her best not to appear sad.

However, it was not long before the King noticed that his third daughter was getting very thin and sad-looking. All of a sudden it flashed through his mind that she had disobeyed his word. To be certain, he called his daughters to him and ordered them to speak the truth. They confessed everything.

The King was so distressed when he heard it that he was almost overcome by grief.

Well, these events had almost been forgotten when one fine day a prince from the East appeared at the court and asked the King for the hand of his eldest daughter. The King gladly gave his consent, and soon after, the happy pair were accompanied to the frontier.

After some time, the same thing happened to the second daughter, who was wooed and won by a prince from the West.

When the young princess saw that everything happened exactly as had been written in the book, she grew very sad. She refused to eat and declared that she would rather die than become a laughingstock to the world. But the King would not allow her to do anything so wrong, and he comforted her in every way.

Now the King was astonished to hear so fine a speech from a pig, and at once it occurred to him that something strange was the matter. When he heard that the court and the whole street were full of all the pigs in the world, the King saw that he must give his consent to the wedding. The pig would not go away till the King had sworn a royal oath upon it.

The King then sent for his daughter and advised her to submit to fate, as there was nothing else to be done. But he added:

"My child, the words and whole behavior of this pig are quite unlike those of other pigs. I do not myself believe that he always was a pig. I think that some magic or witchcraft has been at work. Obey him and do everything that he wishes, and I feel sure that Heaven will shortly reward you."

So the time passed, till lo and behold! one fine day an enormous pig from the North walked into the palace, and going straight up to the King said, "Hail O King! May your life be as prosperous and bright as sunrise on a clear day!"

"I am glad to see you well, friend," answered the King, "but what wind has brought you here?"

"I come a-wooing," replied the pig.

"If you wish me to do this, dear Father, I will do it," replied the girl.

After the marriage, the pig and his bride set out for his home in a royal carriage. On the way, they passed a great bog, and the pig got out and rolled about in the mire till he was covered with mud. Then he got back into the carriage and told his wife to kiss him. She thought of her father's words, and pulling out her pocket handkerchief, she gently wiped the pig's snout and kissed it.

When they reached the pig's dwelling, they had supper together and lay down to rest. During the night, the princess noticed that the pig had changed into a man. She was quite surprised but decided to wait and see what would happen.

And now she noticed that every night the pig became a man, and every morning he was changed into a pig before she awoke. Clearly her husband must be bewitched. In time she grew quite fond of him, he was so kind and gentle.

One day, as she was sitting alone, she saw an old witch go past. She felt quite excited, as it was so long since she had seen a human being. The witch told her that she understood all magic arts, and that she knew the healing powers of herbs and plants.

"Can you tell me," asked the princess, "why my husband is a pig by day and a human by night?"

"If you like, I will give you an herb to break the spell, my dear," said the witch. "At night when your husband is asleep, get up very quietly and fasten this thread round his left foot as firmly as possible. You will see in the morning he will not have changed back into a pig. I do not want any reward. I shall be repaid simply by knowing that you are happy."

When the old witch had gone away, the princess hid the thread very carefully, and at night she got up quietly, and with a beating heart she bound the thread round her husband's foot. Just as she was pulling the knot tight, there was a crack, and the thread broke, for it was rotten.

Her husband awoke and said, "What have you done? Three more days and the unholy spell would have been over. Now, who knows how long I may remain in this shape? I must leave you. We shall not meet again until you have worn out three pairs of iron shoes and blunted a steel staff in your search for me." Then he disappeared.

Now the princess began to weep. But when she saw that her tears did her no good, she got up, determined to go wherever fate should lead her.

On reaching a town, the first thing she did was order three pairs of iron sandals and a steel staff. Then she set out in search of her husband. She wandered over nine seas, across nine continents, and through thick forests; the boughs of the trees hit her face, and the shrubs tore her hands, but on she went. At last, wearied but still with hope in her heart, she reached a house.

Now who do you think lived there? The Moon.

The princess knocked and begged to be let in. The mother of the Moon felt great pity for her and took her in and nursed and tended her. And while she was there, the princess had a little baby.

One day the mother of the Moon asked her:

"How was it possible for a mortal to reach the house of the Moon?"

Then the princess told her all that happened and added: "I shall always be thankful to you. Now I beg one last favor of you; can your daughter, the Moon, tell me where my husband is?"

"She cannot tell you that," replied the goddess, "but, if you will travel toward the East until you reach the dwelling of the Sun, he may be able to tell you something."

Then she gave the princess a roast chicken to eat and warned her to be very careful not to lose any of the bones, because they might be of great use to her.

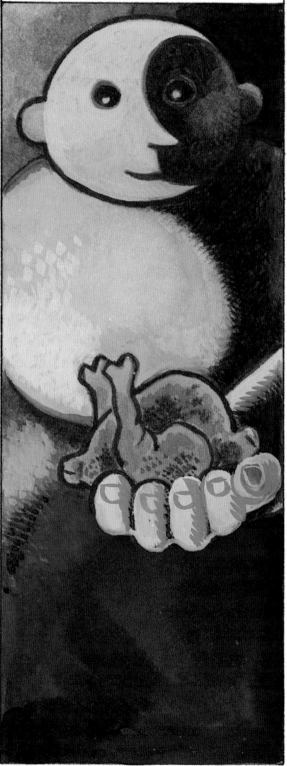

When the princess had thanked
her and had thrown away one pair of
shoes that were worn out, she tied
up the chicken bones in a bundle,
and taking her baby in her arms and
her staff in her hand, she set out
once more.

She went across bare sandy deserts; she crossed high rocky mountains, jumping from crag to crag. She had to cross swamps and to scale mountain peaks covered with sharp rock, so that her feet and knees and elbows were all torn and bleeding. Sometimes she came to a precipice across which she could not jump, and she had to crawl around on hands and knees, helping herself along with her staff.

At length, she reached the palace in which the Sun lived. The mother of the Sun was astonished at beholding a mortal from earth and wept when she heard of all the princess had suffered. Then, having promised to ask her son about the princess's husband, she hid her in the cellar, so that the Sun might notice nothing on his return home, for he was always in a bad temper when he came in at night.

The next day, the princess feared that things would not go well with her, for the Sun had noticed that someone from the other world had been in the palace.

"How in the world is it possible for the Sun to be angry? He is so beautiful and so good to mortals," she asked.

"This is how it happens," replied the Sun's mother. "In the morning, when he stands at the gates of paradise, he is happy and smiles on the whole world, but during the day, he gets cross, because he sees all the evil deeds of men, and that is why his heat becomes so scorching; but in the evening, he is sad and angry, for he stands at the gates of death. Then he comes back here."

She then told the princess that she had asked about her husband, but her son had replied that he knew nothing about him, and that her only hope was to go and inquire of the Wind.

Before the princess left, the mother of the Sun gave her a roast chicken to eat and advised her to take great care of the bones. The princess then threw away her second pair of shoes, which were quite worn out, and with her child on her arm and her staff in her hand, she set forth to find the Wind.

In these wanderings she came
upon one mountain of sharp rocks
after another, out of which tongues
of fire would flame up. She had to
cross fields of ice and avalanches of
snow. The poor woman nearly died
of these hardships, but at length she
reached an enormous cave in the side
of a mountain. This was where the
Wind lived. There was a little door in
front of the cave, and the princess
knocked, begging for admission. The
mother of the Wind had pity on her
and took her in. Here too she was
hidden away, so that the Wind might
not notice her.

The next morning, the mother of the Wind told the princess that her husband was living in a thick woods. There he had built himself a house of tree trunks, and there he lived alone, shunning mankind.

After the mother of the Wind had given the princess a chicken to eat and had warned her to take care of the bones, she advised her to go by the Milky Way, which at night lies across the sky, and to wander until she reached her goal.

Having thanked the old woman, the princess set out and rested neither night nor day, so great was her longing to see her husband.

On and on she walked until her last pair of shoes fell in pieces. So she threw them away and went on with bare feet, not heeding the bogs nor the thorns that wounded her. At last she reached a beautiful, green meadow on the edge of a woods. Her heart was cheered by the sight of the flowers. She sat down and rested a little. But hearing the birds chirping to their mates among the trees made her think with longing of her husband, and she wept bitterly, and taking her child in her arms, she entered the woods.

For three days and three nights she struggled through it. She was quite worn out with weariness and hunger, and even her staff was no further help to her, for it had become quite blunted. She almost gave up but made one last great effort. Suddenly, in a thicket, she came upon the house that the mother of the Wind had described. It had no windows, and the door was up in the roof. Round the house she went in search of steps but could find none. She tried in vain to climb up to the door. Then she thought of the chicken bones that she had dragged all that weary way, and she said to herself: "They would not all have told me to take such good care of these bones if they had not some good reason for doing so."

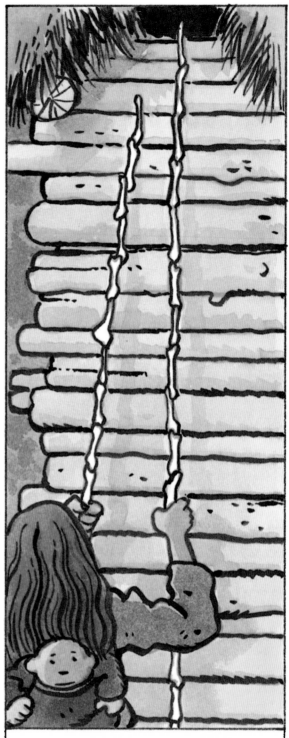

So she took two bones out of her bundle, and she placed the two ends together. To her surprise, they stuck tight. Then she added the other bones till she had two long poles the height of the house; these she placed against the

wall at a distance of a yard from one another. Across them she placed the other bones, piece by piece, like the steps of a ladder. As soon as one step was finished, she stood upon it and made the next one, till she was close to

the door. But just as she got near the top, she noticed that there were no bones left for the last rung of the ladder. Suddenly an idea came to her. Taking a knife, she chopped off her little finger and placed it on the last step,

and it stuck as the bones had done. The ladder was complete, and with her child on her arm, she entered the door of the house. She laid the child down to sleep in a trough that was on the floor and sat down herself to rest.

When her husband, the pig, came back to his house, he could not believe his eyes. He stared at the ladder of bones, and at the little finger on the top of it. He felt that some new magic must be at work, and in his terror, he changed himself into a dove, so that no witchcraft could have power over him. He flew into the room and here he found a woman rocking a child. At the sight of her, looking so changed by all that she had suffered for his sake, his heart was moved by such love and longing and by so great a pity that he suddenly became a man.

The princess stood up when she

saw him, and her heart beat with fear, for she did not know him. But when he told her who he was, in her great joy she forgot all her sufferings, and they seemed as nothing to her. He was a very handsome man. They sat down together and she told him all her adventures, and he wept with pity at the tale. And then he told her his own history.

"I am a king's son. Once when my father was fighting against some dragons, I slew the youngest dragon. His mother, who was a witch, cast a spell and changed me into a pig.

"It was she who gave you the thread to bind round my foot. So that instead of three days, I was forced to remain a pig for three more years. Now that we have suffered for each other, and have found each other again, let us forget the past."

And in their joy they kissed one another.

The next morning, they set out early to return to his father's kingdom. The man's father and mother embraced them both, and there was feasting in the palace for three days and three nights.

Then they set out to see her father. After she had told him all her adventures, he said to her:

"Did I not tell you that I was quite sure the creature who won you as his wife had not been born a pig? You were wise in doing as I told you."

And as the King was old and had no heirs, he put them on the throne in his place. And they ruled as only kings and queens rule who have suffered many things. And if they are not dead, they are still living and ruling happily.

THE FIR TREE

ANDERSEN
ILLUSTRATED BY MARCEL IMSAND
AND RITA MARSHALL

THERE WAS a pretty little fir tree living in a woods. It was in an excellent position, for it could get sun, and there was enough air, and all around grew many tall companions, both pines and firs. The little fir tree's greatest desire was to grow up.

It did not pay attention to the warm sun and the fresh air, or notice the little peasant children who ran about chattering when they came out to gather wild strawberries and raspberries. Often they found a whole basketful and strung strawberries on a straw; they would sit down by the little fir tree and say, "What a pretty little one this is!" The tree did not like that at all.

By the next year it had grown a whole ring taller, and the year after that another ring more, for you can always tell a fir tree's age by its rings.

"Oh, if I were only a great tree like the others," sighed the little fir tree, "then I could stretch out my branches far and wide and look out into the great world! The birds would build their nests in my branches, and when the wind blew, I would bow to it politely just like the others!"

It took no pleasure in the sunshine, nor in the birds, nor in the rose-colored clouds that sailed over it at dawn and at sunset.

Then the winter came, and the snow lay white and sparkling all around, and a hare would come and spring right over the little fir tree, which annoyed it very much. But when two more winters had come and gone, the fir tree was so tall that the hare had to run around it. "Ah, to grow and grow and become great and old! That is the only pleasure in life," thought the tree.

In the autumn, the woodcutters used to come and cut some of the tallest trees. This happened every year, and the young fir tree would shiver as the magnificent trees fell crashing and crackling to the ground, their branches sawed off, and the great trunks left bare, so that they were almost unrecognizable. But then they were laid on wagons and dragged out of the woods by horses. "Where are they going?" the fir tree wondered. "What will happen to them?"

In the spring, when the swallows and storks came, the fir tree asked the birds:

"Do you know where they were taken? Have you met them?"

The swallows knew nothing of them, but the stork nodded his head thoughtfully, saying:

"I think I know. I met many new ships as I flew from Egypt; there were splendid masts on the ships. I'll wager those were they! They had the scent of fir trees. Ah, those are grand, grand!"

"Oh, if I were only big enough to sail away over the sea too! What sort of thing is the sea? What does it look like?"

"Oh, it would take much too long to tell you all that," said the stork, and off he went.

"Rejoice in your youth," said the sunbeams, "rejoice in the sweet growing time, in the young life within you."

And the wind kissed it, and the dew wept tears over it, but the fir tree did not understand.

Toward Christmastime, quite little trees were cut down, some not as big as the young fir tree, or just the same age, and now it had no peace or rest from its longing to be away. These little trees, which were chosen for their beauty, kept all their branches; they were put into carts and drawn out of the woods by horses.

"Where are those going?" asked the fir tree. "They are no bigger than I, and one there was much smaller even! Why do they keep their branches? Where are they taken to?"

"We know! We know!" twittered the sparrows. "Down there in the city we have peeped in through the windows; we know where they go! They come to the greatest splendor and magnificence you can imagine! We have looked in through the windows and seen them planted in the middle of the warm room and adorned with the most beautiful things—golden apples, sweetmeats, toys, and hundreds of candles."

"And then?" asked the fir tree, trembling in every limb, "and then? What happens then?"

"Oh, we haven't seen anything more than that. That was simply matchless!"

"Am I also destined to the same brilliant career?" wondered the fir tree excitedly. "That is even better than sailing over the sea! If it were only Christmas! Now I am tall and grown-up like those that were taken away last year. If I were only in the warm room with all the splendor and magnificence! And then? Then comes something better, something still more beautiful, else why should they dress us up? There must be something grander to come—but what? Oh! I am pining away!"

"Rejoice in us," said the air and sunshine. "Rejoice in your fresh youth in the free air!"

But it took no notice and just grew and grew; there it stood fresh and green in winter and in summer, and all who saw it said, "What a beautiful tree!"

At Christmastime it was the first to be cut down. The axe went deep into the pith. The tree fell to the ground with a groan; it felt bruised and faint and could not think of happiness. It was sad at leaving its home, the spot where it had sprung up; it knew, too, that it would never again see its dear old companions, or the little shrubs and flowers, or perhaps not even the birds.

Altogether the parting was not pleasant.

When the tree came to itself again, it was packed in a yard with other trees, and a man was saying:

"This is a splendid one; we shall only want this."

Then came a man in uniform and carried the fir tree into a large and beautiful room. There were pictures hanging upon the walls, and near the Dutch stove stood great chinese vases with lions on their lids. There were armchairs, silk-covered sofas, big tables laden with picture-books and toys worth hundreds of pounds—at least, so the children said. The fir tree was placed in a great tub filled with sand, but no one could see that it was a tub,

for it was all hung with greenery and stood on a colorful carpet. How the tree trembled! What was coming now? The young ladies and the servants decked it out. On its branches they hung little nets cut out of colored paper, each full of sugarplums. Gilt apples and nuts hung down as if they were growing, and over a hundred red, blue, and white candles were fastened among the branches. Dolls as lifelike as human beings—the fir tree had never seen any before—were suspended among the green, and right up at the top was fixed a golden star. It was gorgeous!

"Tonight," they all said, "tonight it will be lighted!"

"Ah," thought the tree, "if it were only evening! Then the candles would soon be lighted. What will happen then? I wonder whether the trees will come from the woods to see me, or if the sparrows will fly to the window panes? Am I to stand here decked out like this through winter and summer?"

It was not a bad guess, but the fir tree had real bark-ache from sheer longing, and bark-ache in trees is just as bad as a headache in human beings.

Then the candles were lighted. What a glitter! What splendor! The tree quivered in all its branches so much that one of the candles caught the green and singed it. "Take care!" cried the young ladies, and they extinguished it.

Now the tree did not even dare to quiver. It was really terrible! It was so afraid of losing any of its beautiful ornaments, and it was quite bewildered by all the radiance.

And then the folding doors were opened, and a crowd of children rushed in as though they wanted to knock down the whole tree, while the older people followed soberly. The children stood quite silent, but only for a moment, and then they shouted again and danced round the tree and snatched off one present after another.

"What are they doing?" thought the tree. "What is going to happen?" And the candles burnt low on the branches and were put out one by one, and then the children were given permission to plunder the tree. They rushed at it so that all its boughs creaked; if it had not been fastened by the gold star at the top to the ceiling, it would have been knocked over.

The children danced about with their splendid toys, and no one looked at the tree except the old nurse, who came and peeped among the boughs, just to see if a fig or an apple had somehow been forgotten.

"A story, a story!" cried the children, dragging a little stout man to the tree. He sat down beneath it, saying, "Here we are in the greenwood, and the tree will be delighted to listen! But I am only going to tell one story. Shall it be Henny Penny or Humpty Dumpty, who fell down stairs and yet gained great honor and married a princess?"

"Henny Penny!" cried some: "Humpty Dumpty!" cried others; there was such a confusion of voices! Only the fir tree kept silent and thought, "Am I not to be in it? Am I to have nothing to do with it?"

But the fir tree had already been in it and played out its part. And the man told them about Humpty Dumpty, who fell down stairs and married a princess. The children clapped their hands and cried, "Another, another!" They wanted the story of Henny Penny also, but they only got Humpty Dumpty. The fir tree stood quite astonished and thoughtful: the birds in the woods had never related anything like that. "Humpty Dumpty fell down stairs and yet married a princess! Yes, that is the way of the world," thought the tree, and it was sure it must be true, because such a nice man had told the story. "Well, who knows? Perhaps I shall fall down stairs and marry a princess." And it rejoiced to think that the next day it would be decked out again with candles, toys, glittering ornaments, and fruits. "Tomorrow I shall quiver again with excitement. I shall enjoy to the full all my splendor. Tomorrow I shall hear Humpty Dumpty again and perhaps Henny Penny too." And the tree stood silent and lost in thought all through the night.

The next morning, the servants came in. "Now the dressing up will begin again," thought the tree. But they dragged it out of the room, up the stairs to the attic, and put it in a dark corner, where no ray of light could penetrate. "What does this mean?" thought the tree. "What am I to do here? What is there for me to hear?" And it leaned against the wall and thought and thought. And there was time enough for that, for many days and nights went by, and no one came. At last when someone did come, it was only to put some great boxes into the corner. Now the tree was covered; it seemed as if it had been forgotten.

"Now it is winter outdoors," thought the fir tree. "The ground is hard and covered with snow, they can't plant me yet, and that is why I am staying here under cover till the spring comes. How thoughtful they are! Only I wish it were not so terribly dark and lonely here; not even a little hare! It was so nice out in the woods, when the snow lay all around and the hare leaped past me; yes, even when he leaped over me. It's so dreadfully lonely up here."

"Squeak, squeak!" said a little mouse, stealing out, followed by a second. They sniffed at the fir tree and then crept between its boughs. "It's frightfully cold," said the little mice. "How nice it is to be here! Don't you think so too, you old fir tree?"

"I'm not at all old," said the tree. "There are many much older than I am."

"Where do you come from?" asked the mice, "and what do you know?" They were extremely inquisitive. "Do tell us about the most beautiful place in the world. Is that where you come from? Have you been in the storeroom, where cheeses lie on the shelves, and hams hang from the ceiling, where one dances on tallow candles, and where one goes in thin and comes out fat?"

"I know nothing about that," said the tree. "But I know the woods, where the sun shines and the birds sing." And then it told them all about its young days, and the little mice cried: "Oh, how much you have seen! How lucky you have been!"

"I?" said the fir tree, and then it thought over what it had told them. "Yes, on the whole, those were very happy times." But then it went on to tell them about Christmas Eve, when it had been so beautifully adorned.

"Oh!" said the little mice. "How lucky you have been, you old fir tree!"

"I'm not at all old," said the tree. "I only came from the woods this winter. I am only a little delayed, perhaps, in my growth."

"How beautifully you tell stories!" said the little mice. And next evening they came with four others who wanted to hear the tree's story, and it told still more, for it remembered everything so clearly and thought, "Those were happy times! But they may come again. Humpty Dumpty fell down stairs, and yet he married a princess; perhaps I shall also marry a princess!" And then it thought of a pretty little birch tree that grew out in the woods and seemed to the fir tree a real princess and a very beautiful one too.

"Who is Humpty Dumpty?" asked the little mice.

And then the tree told the whole story. It could remember every single word, and the little mice were ready to leap on the topmost branch out of sheer joy!

The next night many more mice came, and on Sunday even two rats showed up. But the rats did not care about the story, and that troubled the little mice, because now they thought less of it too.

"Is that the only story you know?" asked the rats.

"The only one," answered the tree. "I heard that on my happiest evening, but I did not realize then how happy I was."

"That is a very poor story. Don't you know one about bacon or tallow candles? A storeroom story?"

"No," said the tree.

"Then thank you anyway," said the rats, and they went back to their friends.

At last the little mice went off also, and the tree said, sighing: "Really it was very pleasant when the lively little mice sat around and listened while I told them stories. But now that's over too.

But now I will think of the time when I shall be brought out again to keep up my spirits."

But when did that happen? Well, it was one morning when people came to tidy up the attic; the boxes were set aside, and the tree brought out. They threw it really rather roughly on the floor, but a servant dragged it off at once downstairs, where there was daylight once more.

"Now life begins again," thought the tree. It felt the fresh air, the first rays of the sun, and there it was out in the yard! Everything passed so quickly; the tree quite forgot to notice itself, there was so much to look at all around. The yard opened on a garden full of flowers; the roses were so fresh and sweet, hanging over a little trellis. The lime trees were in blossom, and the swallows flew about, saying, "Quirre-virre-vit, my husband has come home." But it was not the fir tree they meant.

"Now I shall live," thought the tree joyfully, stretching out its branches wide. But, alas, they were all withered and yellow; and it was lying in a corner among weeds and nettles. The golden star was still on its highest bough, and it glittered in the bright sunlight. In the yard, some of the merry children who had danced so happily around the tree at Christmas were playing. One of the little ones ran up and tore off the gold star.

"Look what was left on the ugly old fir tree!" he cried and stomped on the boughs so that they cracked under his feet.

And the tree looked at all the splendor and freshness of the flowers in the garden and then looked at itself and wished that it had been left lying in the dark corner of the attic; it thought of its fresh youth in the woods, of the merry Christmas Eve, and of the little mice who had

listened so happily to the story of Humpty Dumpty.

"Too late! Too late!" thought the old tree. "If only I had enjoyed myself while I could. Now all is over and gone."

And a servant came and cut the tree into small pieces. There was quite a bundle of them, and they flickered brightly in the flames under a great copper kettle. The tree sighed deeply, and each sigh was like a pistol shot; so the children who were playing there ran up and sat in front of the fire, gazing at it and crying, "Pfiff! puff! bang!" But for each report, which was really a sigh, the tree was thinking of a summer's day in the woods, or of a winter's night out there, when the stars were shining. It thought of Christmas Eve and of Humpty Dumpty, which was the only story it had heard, or could tell, and then the tree burned away.

The children played on in the garden, and the youngest had the golden star on his chest—the star the tree had worn on the happiest evening of its life. And now that was past—and the tree had passed away—and the story too, all ended and done with.

And that's the way with all stories!

Beauty & the Beast

Few fairy tales have enjoyed such wide-spread and long-lasting popularity as *Beauty & the Beast*. The earliest written version of this story was created in 1637 by an Italian named Giambattista Basile. In the decades that followed, a number of other writers penned their own versions. When Madame Gabrielle de Villeneuve published a French version in 1740, it was three hundred and sixty-two pages long. Literary experts believe that Villeneuve based her story on *Le Mouton*, a tale written in the early 1700s by another French court lady and author named Madame d'Aulnoy.

Over the next century and a half, the story was greatly shortened. In 1889, *Beauty & the Beast* was published in English in *The Blue Fairy Book*, a collection of folktales compiled by scholar Andrew Lang. The story continued to grow in popularity in the 1900s, spawning numerous movies and stage musicals. Though *Beauty & the Beast* has appeared in many languages and versions over the past four centuries, its message has never changed: true beauty lies within.

About the Illustrator

Etienne Delessert is the creator of more than eighty children's books. His delightful and thought-provoking illustrations have won him nine gold and six silver medals from the Society of Illustrators. He has also been awarded twice with the Premio Grafico from the Bologna Children's Book Fair. His illustrations in such titles as *Dance!* and *Ashes, Ashes* have established his international reputation as one of the fathers of modern children's picture books. He now lives in Connecticut with his wife and son.

Cinderella

The search for true love is the driving element of many classic fairy tales. *Cinderella* is perhaps the best known of such stories. Oral storytelling in Europe reached its high point in the Middle Ages, and *Cinderella* was among the tales told in ballad form by traveling minstrels. Highly popular, versions of *Cinderella* soon spread across Europe and the Middle East, eventually reaching all the way to China.

Charles Perrault, a scholar of French folktales, was the first person to write down many of the stories told through Europe's oral tradition. *Cendrillon, ou la petite pantoufle de verre* (*Cinderella; or, The Little Glass Slipper*) was thus included in *Contes de ma Mère l'Oye* (*Tales of Mother Goose*), a book of well-known tales published by Perrault in 1697. The book was a huge success and inspired other literary scholars to collect and translate fairy tales from all parts of Europe. One such scholar was Andrew Lang, who included *Cinderella* in *The Blue Fairy Book*, the famous anthology that was published in 1889 and has never been out of print since.

About the Illustrator

Roberto Innocenti was born in Bagno a Ripoli, a small town near Florence, Italy. Never receiving any formal art training, he began his career designing film and theater posters and has since become one of the world's foremost children's book illustrators. His artwork in such books as *Nutcracker* and *Pinocchio* has won a number of prestigious awards, including the American Library Association Notable Children's Book and the Bratislava Golden Apple Award. He now lives in Florence with his wife.

Hansel & Gretel

For centuries, fairy tales were a major part of Europe's oral tradition. Told and retold, then written and rewritten, fairy tales are now one of the oldest surviving forms of literature. In the early 1800s, German brothers Jakob and Wilhelm Grimm set out to preserve the stories of this tradition, traveling throughout Europe and copying down fairy tales recited to them. In 1810, Wilhelm penned the first written version of *Hansel & Gretel* as told to him by an old storyteller living in a forest village in Northern Germany.

Hansel & Gretel appeared in print in 1812 in the first volume of the brothers' *Kinder- und Hausmärchen* (*Children's and Household Tales*). As with all of *Grimm's Fairy Tales*, as the tales would collectively become known, the brothers continually revised the story for new editions of their books. Volume two of *Children's and Household Tales* appeared in 1814, and a revised *Hansel & Gretel* was among one hundred and fifty-six stories printed within its pages. Since then, this classic tale has been published in various forms in more than forty countries.

About the Illustrator

Swiss artist Monique Felix studied graphic arts at l'Ecole des Arts Appliqués de Lausanne. Since starting out in advertising design, she has illustrated more than forty children's picture books. Among her notable illustrated books are the award-winning *Mouse Books* series, *Tuba Lessons*, and *Hundreds of Fish*. Her picture book artwork has been honored with numerous awards, including the Bratislava Golden Apple Award and the Octogone Prize from the International Center of Children's Literature in France.

The Three Languages

The Three Languages was first put into print by the Brothers Grimm in the early 1800s. But various cultures were telling their own versions of this tale long before then. In one version taken from Russia's early oral tradition, it is a bear rather than a pack of dogs that guards a great treasure. And it is a pair of golden hawks instead of doves who lead the hero to his rightful place, not as the Pope in Rome but as the ruler of a vast mountaintop kingdom.

As folktales and fairy tales evolved in many regions of Europe, they sometimes adopted religious lessons. It was in Central Europe during the 1700s that *The Three Languages* evolved to have the hero travel to Rome, where he becomes Pope. Such an event served as a lesson in righteousness and its rewards to young listeners of the tale. Readers first enjoyed a written version of this tale in *Kinder- und Hausmärchen* (*Children's and Household Tales*), the famed collection published by the Brothers Grimm.

About the Illustrator

Ivan Chermayeff is among America's most prominent painters and designers. He has been honored with his own exhibition at the Ricco/Maresca Gallery, and his work has been displayed in the Smithsonian's Museum of American History. He has also produced commissioned paintings, murals, and sculptures for major corporations for nearly three decades. Among the numerous honors he has received is a Gold Medal from the American Institute of Graphic Arts.

The Fisherman & His Wife

The Fisherman & His Wife, a simple but classic lesson of the dangers of greed, is today one of the most adored stories in children's literature. The tale originated centuries ago in the folktale tradition involving enchanted animals who are captured and forced to grant wishes. In early Russian tales, the animal was a bear or a reindeer; in China, the magical creature was a dragon. But one theme remained constant in all versions of the story: greed begets suffering.

The earliest written form of this story has its roots in *The Book of the Subtyle Historyes and Fables of Esope* (*The Fables of Aesop*), a collection of stories published in 1481 by William Caxton, the man who established England's first printing press. Caxton's anthology contained several stories that inspired the original writer of *The Fisherman & His Wife*, romantic painter Philipp Otto Runge. In 1809, Runge's version made its way into the hands of the Brothers Grimm, who translated the tale and included it in *Kinder- und Hausmärchen* (*Children's and Household Tales*) in 1812.

About the Illustrator

John Howe was born in British Columbia and attended l'Ecole des Arts Décoratifs de Strasbourg. The illustrator of many children's books, he is also a renowned Tolkien artist whose incredible balance of reality and fantasy has garnered worldwide acclaim. He has created conceptual art for such motion pictures as the *Lord of the Rings* movie trilogy and illustrated such prominent books as the Time-Life series *The Enchanted World*. He currently lives in Switzerland with his wife and son.

The Queen Bee

One of the earliest versions of *The Queen Bee* dates back to sixteenth-century China, a culture with a rich oral tradition of animal tales. Over the next two centuries, several versions of the story appeared in Eastern Europe. In the early 1800s, Jakob and Wilhelm Grimm compiled their impressive collection of folktales and fairy tales that was published as *Kinder- und Hausmärchen* (*Children's and Household Tales*). *The Queen Bee* was included in this collection, which came to contain more than two hundred stories.

The Brothers Grimm continually revised their stories for new editions of *Children's and Household Tales*, which were published every few years. However, *The Queen Bee* is one of the few tales that remains very close to the original Eastern European form that the brothers first discovered, maintaining its simple moral about the repayment of good deeds. Since it was first published by the Brothers Grimm, *The Queen Bee* has remained in print and has even made its way back to China.

About the Illustrator

Philippe Dumas was born in Cannes, France, and studied theater design, painting, and illustration at l'Ecole des Beaux-arts de Paris. Since his first children's book, *Laura, Alice's New Land*, was published in 1976, he has illustrated many more books in Europe and the United States, including *The Farm*. In 1987, he was awarded the coveted Grand Prix of Children's Literature by the city of Paris for his body of work. He now lives in Switzerland.

Bushy Bride

Originating from Norway's rich oral tradition centuries ago, *Bushy Bride* imparts a basic moral lesson about the rewards of kindness and the punishment of ill temper. Because the rivers, lakes, and seas of the northland factored heavily into the lives of the people of Norway, *Bushy Bride* is one of many Norwegian stories involving travel over the sea and water-going creatures. In a popular Finnish and Swedish version of *Bushy Bride*, the three-headed creature emerges from a cave instead of a brook.

Although many English and French stories were written down by the 1600s, the folktales of Norway remained unprinted until 1845, when Norwegian scholars Peter Christian Asbjörnsen and Jörgen E. Moe collected many of the stories originally told in their native land and published them in a book called *Norwegian Folk Tales*. The two men were inspired to collect these stories, which included *Bushy Bride*, by a renewed interest in ancient cultural history and folklore that was sweeping across Scandinavia and Northern Europe. The story has changed very little since that time.

About the Illustrator

Renowned illustrator and graphic designer Seymour Chwast was born in New York City in 1931. He has created more than thirty children's books, and his illustrated posters have been exhibited in a number of major international galleries and museums, including the Museum of Modern Art and the Louvre. In the 1950s, he co-founded Push Pin Studios and remains the director of the studio today. In 1985, he was honored with a Gold Medal from the American Institute of Graphic Arts.

The Sleeping Beauty

The quest for true love has always been at the heart of some of the best-loved folktales and fairy tales, and few stories embody this timeless theme like *The Sleeping Beauty*. The earliest written version of this story was created by Italian poet and soldier Giambattista Basile and published in 1637. However, literary scholars believe that Giambattista's story was actually derived from a 1528 romance story based on the ancient Greek legend of the prince Troylus and princess Zellandine.

In the mid-1600s, Frenchman Charles Perrault began collecting and translating folktales and fairy tales from around the world. Perrault changed Basile's version considerably, adding detail to the relationships between the story's characters. *La Belle au Bois Dormant* (*The Sleeping Beauty in the Wood*) thus became the familiar tale known today. This story of jealousy and love, so admired by readers everywhere, was later included in the famous fairy tale collections published by the Brothers Grimm and Andrew Lang.

About the Illustrator

John Collier is among America's most respected illustrators. His works in oils and pastels have earned fourteen gold medals from the Society of Illustrators and the prestigious Hamilton King award. They have also been displayed in the Smithsonian Museum, the New York Historical Society, and other prominent galleries around the world. *The Sleeping Beauty* is one of three children's books he has illustrated. He now lives in Texas with his wife.

The Enchanted Pig

The Enchanted Pig hails from the classic tradition of transformation tales—stories that involve magic spells and transfigurations and often emphasize the value of looking beyond appearances. Originally part of Hungary's ancient oral tradition, *The Enchanted Pig* is one of the world's oldest fairy tales. Creative storytelling was deeply treasured in Hungary during the mid-1400s. But when the country fell to the Turks in the 1500s, folktales and other cultural traditions collapsed with it.

Fortunately, a few people kept the art of storytelling alive, and *The Enchanted Pig* never fully disappeared. Two hundred years after the Turks' invasion, a freed Hungary and the new nation of Rumania (which had once been part of Hungary) reclaimed many of the region's literary traditions, including the telling of *The Enchanted Pig*. The tale, which has since become a staple of Rumanian children's literature, did not appear in print until 1858, when it was included in the book *Antologie de Basm* (*Anthology of Fairy Stories*).

About the Illustrator

Jacques Tardi was born in France in 1946 and studied graphic arts at the l'Ecole des beaux-arts de Lyon. He began his career illustrating French comics and went on to both write and illustrate an array of books, many of which are World War I stories or detective mysteries. Among his best-known works is the classic collection of war portraits *C'était la Guerre des Tranchées* (*That Was Trench Warfare*). His distinctive clear line style of illustration has earned the admiration of critics worldwide.

The Fir Tree

Most well-known folktales and fairy tales began as oral stories that were eventually written down by such writers as Charles Perrault and the Brothers Grimm. But Danish author Hans Christian Andersen wrote original fairy tales based on his own experiences, creating one of the world's greatest literary legacies. After publishing his first collection of stories in 1835, Andersen published a second collection a decade later. It was this second anthology—simply called *Eventyr* (*Fairy Tales*)—that included *The Fir Tree*, a timeless tale of regrets and missed opportunities.

Because Andersen's work was so popular in its native land of Denmark, it was only a matter of time before the rest of the world took notice of his remarkable talent. Andersen made his first trip to England in 1847, just two years after *The Fir Tree* first appeared in print, and became friends with Charles Dickens and other great English writers. Since then, Andersen's enduring tales have inspired countless storytellers and filmmakers, who have adapted many of his works in various forms.

About the Illustrators

Marcel Imsand was born in Switzerland in 1929. He worked as a mechanic until deciding at the age of thirty-five to pursue photography. The career move was a brilliant one, and he has become known as one of Switzerland's finest photographers. With more than fifty photographic books to his credit, he has received such international honors as a bronze medal in the 1985 Leipzig Most Beautiful Books in the World Competition.

After working as an art director for advertising agencies in Denver, Rita Marshall moved to Switzerland in 1981 and began designing books for children and adults. As an author she has written *I Hate to Read*, winner of the 1993 Benjamin Franklin Award. Her work has earned international acclaim, including gold and silver medals from the Society of Illustrators and the New York Art Director's Club. She has also been awarded the Bologna Children's Book Fair Premio Grafico four times. She currently lives in Connecticut with her husband and son.